Evernight Publishing

www.evernightpublishing.com

Copyright© 2013

Evernight Publishing

ISBN: 978-1-77130-631-7

Editor: Dana Horbach

Cover Artist: LF Designs

COVERT MISSION: UNDERCOVER COP

DEDICATION

This book is dedicated to my three wonderful and supportive sons:

Christopher, Nicholas and Joshua.

Without them, my life would mean nothing.

Love you guys!

Mom
xoxoxo

Covert Mission: Undercover Cop

Thunder Creek Ranch, 2

Lorraine Nelson

Copyright © 2011

Chapter One

"What on Earth have you packed in this one?" Blake said as he hefted a box to go to the truck.

"If I can pack it and stack it, you've got nothing worth complaining about," said Samantha in that brusque "don't mess with me" tone she used around most people. Since losing her arm and receiving a medical discharge from the army, Sam fought harder than ever to prove her self-sufficiency, especially around men.

"I'm not, but a word of warning wouldn't come amiss."

"So sorry, Blake. I'll be sure to label the heavy ones as 'women weight only' from now on."

"Huh! I don't believe you could lift it yourself, let alone carry it all the way to the truck."

That did it! "What's your wager?" She thrived on their little wagers. Blake was so much fun to tease and a good loser to boot.

"Dinner, Friday night. Loser pays."

"Throw in a movie and you've got a deal." This was a sure bet. She'd enjoy his company and not have to spend Friday night alone.

"Dinner and a movie it is," he smirked, handing the box off to Sam.

"Great! I'll look forward to a relaxing evening since it seems I have to handle all the heavy work around here." Smiling, she waltzed out through the kitchen door and met Luke, Blake's friend, on his way back in. She'd met both men through her friend, Zakia. Luke and Zakia had recently remarried after an estrangement of several years and she and Blake had offered to help her move.

"Here, Sam. I can take that for you."

"Not on your life, cowboy. This box in the truck gets me dinner and a movie."

"You and Blake at it again?"

"Of course!" She chuckled.

"Why don't you cut him a little slack? He's only trying to be a gentleman."

"That may well be, but I get a rise out of him so easy I can't resist."

"What would you do if he asked you out on a real date?"

"What?" she shrieked. "He wouldn't. Blake knows I don't date."

"Uh, huh. Ain't that the truth."

"Well, he does."

"I know, Sam. Far be it from me to thwart your 'no dating' scene."

"What do you mean by that?" she called back as she set the box down on the tailgate of Luke's truck.

"Nothing much, but for two people who aren't dating, you sure seem to go out a lot." He chuckled, walking inside and letting the door swing shut behind him.

Sam stood and stared after him for a moment, thinking about what he'd said. He was right. She did accompany Blake on a lot of outings, but they were friends. Why shouldn't they attend functions and things together? It beat going alone. And he was good company.

Still, if people were starting to talk—classifying them as a couple—she shuddered, maybe it was time to back off. She didn't want *him* to get the wrong idea. Didn't want to have to explain…nope! Not going there. The past was right where it belonged, in the past. She'd dealt with it and made her choice. There was no turning back but still, she couldn't ward off a niggling doubt.

Blake came out of the house carrying another carton of Zakia's things. Her gaze tracked his movements. He sure was a handsome devil.

He greeted her with a disarming grin. "So you made it to the truck, I see."

"Yes, I did, but then, you knew I would," she said, suddenly realizing it as the truth when Blake's face turned red.

"How could I know? That box was damned heavy." He turned to load his box on the truck. "I do like the way you rise to a challenge though."

"Is that so?"

He straightened to face her, his smile bordering on a smirk. "Yep, so we're on for Friday night?"

"Nope. At least, not this Friday. I'm busy."

Blake scowled, his expression stating that he was not pleased with her reply. "Doing what?"

She thought fast. "The shop needs painting, so when I close for the weekend, I'll need to get at it."

"I can help."

"If I needed your help, I'd ask for it. Haven't you figured that out by now?"

"Well, excuse me if I'm trying to be neighborly."

"That's another thing." His eyes flared—with anger? Something else? She softened her tone, not wanting to appear ungrateful. "We're not exactly neighbors. For someone who lives an hour away, you seem to be in Calgary a lot these days. What gives?"

"You know I'm collaborating on Grayson's case. Why do you ask?"

"Every Friday?" she asked, a skeptical tone in her voice.

"Yeah, it gets me out of the office. Why all the questions?"

Could that really be all there was to it? "Just that I don't want you going out of your way to help me. I don't like owing anybody anything."

He walked closer, close enough to touch, but he didn't. She waited, knowing he had something to say and wished he'd just get it over with.

"You don't owe me anything. Is it so hard for you to accept that I enjoy spending time with you?"

Yes! No! She schooled her features into a polite mask. "I don't know."

"I thought we were friends."

"We are, but people are starting to talk."

"About us? Is that so bad?" he asked in that low, sexy voice of his.

"Blake, you know I don't date. I don't do relationships and commitment. Friendship is all I can handle. All I'll ever have to offer." She fought to keep her eyes from tearing up. No way would she cry in front of this man or anyone else for that matter. Zakia wasn't even privy to her darkest secrets. She was a rough, tough, independent woman and intended to keep it that way.

"I think you're cutting yourself short, Sam. Life is for living."

"And I'm living it my way. I thought you understood." She started to walk away then turned and looked back, catching his concerned yet puzzled expression. "Come on. Get your ass in gear, Northrup. We have more boxes to pack and lug."

"Yes, ma'am!" He saluted her then caught up in time to open the door for her.

She accepted the gesture gracefully for once, knowing she'd already spouted off enough for one day.
* * * *

Blake went back to helping Zakia pack and move, constantly wondering what all the fuss was about with Sam. He'd tried to be the perfect gentleman, but that didn't seem to work with her. She was as independent and as prickly as they came. They were friends, sure, but he'd been hoping for so much more.

From the first time he'd laid eyes on her, he knew she was the woman for him. Sam had arrived at The Thunder Creek Ranch, his friend Luke's spread, and he'd glanced out the window in time to see her emerging from her Chevy Tracker, which was painted up in camouflage detail. Hair as dark as midnight, cut short and curled toward her face in a sassy, don't take no crap style, didn't take anything away from the long-legged beauty encased in skintight blue jeans and long-sleeved shirt. His erection had been swift and painful.

He'd gotten to know her fairly well over those few weeks at the ranch, but she had a "no dating" rule that may as well be etched in concrete. They'd spent a lot of time together, then and since, but his innuendoes had been for nothing. She ignored them, insisted on being *just* friends.

He loved taking her places and showing her a good time. She was intelligent, witty, and sexy as hell, but he was tired of being pushed away before he'd even gotten close. Maybe it was time to back off and give her a little breathing room. Would she miss him if he did? Or would she shrug and get on with her life, forgetting his existence?

"I think that's all we can fit in this load," said Luke as he came up behind him, loading another box on the back and shoving the tailgate closed. "Let's grab the girls and head to the ranch."

"You can alert the women. I still need to secure the load on my truck before we leave."

"Okay, buddy. Back in a sec."

Blake had closed the trunk on Zakia's Caddy, shut the back hatch on Sam's tracker, and tied down the load on his four by four Dodge Ram by the time his friends joined him. The trip to Luke's gave him plenty of time to think, but the thoughts kept rolling around in his head without conclusion. He still hadn't formulated a plan of action by the time they arrived and had to unload everything.

"What's up, Blake? You haven't uttered a word since we arrived," said Luke.

"That's because you're keeping me too busy to form a coherent sentence," he joked.

"Are you too tired to smile? You're not your usual self. Is it Sam?"

Blake perched a hip on the tailgate and breathed a long, drawn out sigh. His friend knew him well enough. "Yeah, it's Sam. What else? That woman is going to be the death of me."

"What happened?"

"She's worried about people thinking we're a couple. Reminded me that she doesn't date, that we're just friends. I'm not sure how much more *friendship* I can take."

"Oops! Sorry, buddy. That's probably my fault."

"How so?"

"She told me about your current wager and I commented, something like, for a person who doesn't date, you two sure go out a lot."

"Yep, that would do it." He wasn't annoyed with Luke, rather thankful that his friend had been brave enough to confront Sam. Maybe it was time he stopped playing by the books. "The thing is, I'm not sure if it's just me or if she really doesn't want to get involved with anybody. Is she holding me off thinking she'll meet her Mr. Right someday?"

"Have you tried asking her?"

"Not in so many words. I'm not sure I'm ready to hear the answer."

"Tough call, but you'll handle it. I say ask her. Put your questions out there and see what happens."

He glanced toward the house and saw Samantha headed their way. "Nope, not yet." He didn't want to totally blow his chances. If she said no…. "I'll figure it out, but thanks for listening."

"Anytime, Blake. Now let's finish unloading. Zakia's rustling up some lunch and I'm starving."

"Sounds good." He lifted a couple boxes and passed Sam on the way to the house. She nodded and smiled so he did the same. *Friends!* Humph! He had many friends, male and female, but none of them caused the reactions this one did. For his own sanity, when this day was over he would keep to himself if it killed him, which it probably would.

* * * *

13

"Well, that's the last of it." Luke stretched as they met in the upstairs hallway.

"Those twins sure have a passel of toys." Blake gestured to the pile of boxes they'd hauled. "When do they find time to play with them all?"

Luke laughed. "I don't know. I built them a sandbox around by the swings, but once the novelty wore off, they were back to playing with the puppies. I'm glad the police finally gave the okay for us to clear out her place in town though. This makes it permanent."

"I thought retaking your vows made it permanent," teased Blake. He'd been best man again with Sam as the Maid of Honor. He bit back a groan as he recalled her form-fitting dress, showing off more than a hint of cleavage.

"Yeah, but I wanted the boys and Zakia to have their own stuff here. Did you see all those cookbooks?"

That brought his attention back. "*See* them? Sam and I lugged them out to the truck."

Luke laughed. "We'll have to have you out for dinner one of these days."

"Let me know when." Blake smiled. "If she catered for a living she must be a damn good cook."

"Speaking of Cook, are you coming out for the last cookout of the season?"

"Wouldn't miss it. This coming weekend, right?"

"Yep, Saturday afternoon and evening. Cook's doing dinner, but Zakia and Winnie are making the desserts."

"My mouth is watering already. Is there anything else you need help with today?"

Luke looked over his shoulder at the piles of boxes stored in the spare room and groaned. "No, it's just a matter of unpacking and rearranging stuff now, but Zakia will work on it as she has time."

"All right. I'm going to shove off, check in at the station, and make sure everything's been running smooth in my absence." He turned and headed for the stairs, not stopping until he'd reached the front entry.

"Okay. Thanks for all your help today. You're welcome to stay and sit a spell, have dinner with us."

Blake hesitated, part of him wanting to see Sam one last time, part of him needing to avoid another encounter. "Another time, Luke. See you on Saturday." He exited through the front door and took the steps two at a time. His lengthy stride soon carried him to his truck. Without looking back, afraid he'd change his mind and open himself to more heartache, he fired up the engine and accelerated down the driveway.

* * * *

"Where's he off to in such a hurry?" asked Sam as she stepped up beside Luke and watched Blake drive away.

"Said he had to check in at the station."

"Oh! Is he…uh…coming back for dinner?"

"Nope. I was just going to do the evening chores. Did you want something?"

"No, I'm fine, Luke. Just needed a breath of fresh air. You go."

She watched as he walked away. Zakia sure got lucky with that one. He doted on her and those twins of theirs. With another one, or two, on the way, they couldn't be happier. She grinned, happy for them.

That kind of life was not for her, no matter how much she longed for it. No home and hearth in the foreseeable future. Not her future anyway. Her gaze traveled the length of the driveway, dust clouds starting to disperse after Blake's hasty departure.

He hadn't even said good-bye, which wasn't like him at all. She felt a definite pang in her chest at the thought. He'd always sought her out for the flimsiest of reasons. Had she taken his attention for granted? Had she come on too strong today in insisting they remain just friends?

She considered him a real good friend. He had a great sense of humor, a chivalrous attitude and charming to boot. His companionship had brought her to realize that she was still a woman with a woman's wants and needs. It did her heart good to be with such a handsome man. And it wasn't vanity on her part, more a sense of flagging self-confidence in her worth. Blake made her feel sexy and alive for the first time since her discharge.

The screen door slammed shut behind her as Zakia's twin boys came running outside.

"Where's Daddy?" Casey asked.

"He just went to the barn."

Without another word, they were off and running across the ranch yard. They didn't seem to miss the city at all, fitting in at the ranch as if they'd been raised here. She understood the sentiment. She loved it here, too. So much beauty in the surrounding landscape and a peace the likes she'd never encountered anywhere else, especially since Zakia's stalker, Roy Grayson, was behind bars.

That bastard had caused a heap of trouble all around. She wondered how Winnie and Lucas Senior were coping. Having her son arrested for a crime against her husband's family had to put quite a strain on their marriage.

The hinges protested as the screen door opened again, the squeak alerting her that she was no longer alone.

"Hi, Sam! I heard the slamming door and thought the boys came this way," Zakia said as glanced around.

"They did, but were looking for Luke. I told them he was in the barn and they went running."

"Oh, good! I can sit for a moment without worrying about them getting into stuff. Their method of unpacking is to open all the boxes and drag the contents out onto the floor. It'll take me a good week or two to sort out their room."

Sam laughed, loving the hearty exuberance of the two little boys. She loved kids and these two were special, but.... "They're just excited at the move. Give it a day or two and they'll calm down."

"I'm just glad Mom and Dad took them during the bulk of the move. Did I tell you they had a going away party for them?"

"No! Really?"

"Yep! Had a houseful of little monsters all afternoon. They were exhausted yet smiling when I picked up the boys."

"That was thoughtful of them."

"Yeah, but the surplus of cake and ice cream has them wound for sound." Zakia let loose a heavy sigh as she sat in the rocker.

Sam grinned. "Those boys never walk when they can run. How are you holding up, Zak?" she asked, concerned because her friend had so much to do and pregnant too.

"Tired, but I'm glad everything's here."

"Want me to help organize the boys' room?"

"Not tonight, but can you stay over? It would be great to at least have that done."

"Let me check with Brogan. If he'll tend the shop again tomorrow, I'm all yours."

"Thanks, Sam. You're the best!"

"Not the best," she muttered to herself, "but I'll do." She'd never been best at anything in her life. Joining the army had been a good move, she'd excelled at her duties there, but look how that had ended. She had been strong enough and determined enough to overcome her physical disabilities, but emotionally, not so much.

She wanted Blake…wanted to be with him. This fierce ache inside wouldn't go away on its own, but she was afraid, terribly afraid, that she'd end up hurt and alone again. No man in his right mind would commit to half a woman, and that's exactly how she felt. Better to keep her needs in check and have his friendship than to try for something more and lose him altogether.

"What was that?" Zakia asked.

"Nothing, just thinking out loud. Here come Luke and the boys. Looks like your rest is over." She turned to her friend. "Are you happy, Zak? Truly happy?"

"Yes, Sam. I should never have left. Luke is the only man I've ever wanted."

The two women watched as Zakia's husband and children crossed the ranch yard, playing a kind of leapfrog where one ran ahead, then the other, all three participating until they reached the front porch steps.

"Hello, beautiful," Luke said as he bent to kiss Zakia. "What's for dinner?"

The twins giggled. Sam smiled. She was so happy for her friend. Zakia was such an open and giving person, committed to her life with Luke. If only she could be like that.

"Cook said he'd send something over. Doesn't want me overdoing things."

"Smart man," said Luke. "Remind me to give him a raise. Come on, boys. We need to wash up before our grub gets here."

The boys followed him into the house without argument, and the porch suddenly became quiet.

"Zak, I think I'll head back to town, get a few things cleared away. I don't think there'll be any problems with me taking another day off, so I'll drive back down in the morning."

"Why not just stay? We have plenty of room."

"Nah! Third wheel and all that. I like driving, gives me time to think."

Zak hesitated as if she wanted to argue the point but nodded instead. "Okay, if you're sure, but I can tackle the room by myself if you don't make it back, so don't worry."

"I won't. Say bye to the kids for me and you take it easy tonight."

"Aren't you staying for dinner?"

"Nope, going to hit the road. I'll pick up a bite when I get to town."

"Sam, are you all right?" Zakia asked, concern evident in her expression.

"I'm fine, just need to do some thinking, which isn't possible with those twins of yours around." She smiled to take any sting out of her words. "I'll see you in the morning. Bye, Zak."

"Bye, Sam. Drive safe."

"Always do." She slid in behind the wheel, thoughts of Blake taking over before she'd cleared the end of the driveway.

She purposely drove by the station in Fort McLeod on her way out of town and, seeing Blake's four-by-four, she hesitated then hit the accelerator. Better to leave things as they were. If she knew Blake, he'd show up with paintbrush in hand on Friday. They'd talk then.

COVERT MISSION: UNDERCOVER COP

Chapter Two

Paperwork had piled up in his absence, so Blake tackled it to keep his mind off Sam. Roy Grayson's preliminary hearing was set for Monday morning, and he intended to be there. He read through a copy of the statements on file, but he really didn't need to. The details were embedded in his brain, having been on hand for most of the scoundrel's shenanigans. It still frustrated him to no end that he'd gotten to Zakia even with all the precautions they'd taken. *Sneaky bastard!*

The fact that Sam could've been seriously hurt while protecting her friend wasn't lost on him either. If Roy had administered the wrong dosage of tranq juice, she might be six feet under by now. His gut twisted at the thought. Yep, he'd definitely attend that hearing.

He heard a vehicle slow down out front and glanced out the window to see Sam's Chevy Tracker, but instead of stopping, she sped up and drove past. What was that all about? The station wasn't anywhere near her route home. Had she been coming to see him and changed her mind? Maybe he should go after her. Nope! He'd decided to stay away from her for now. If she wanted to talk to him, let her do the running for a change. There was only so much rejection a man could take.

Although she hadn't really rejected him. It was more like she preferred keeping their relationship platonic. And for the life of him, he couldn't understand why. They'd been together quite often since they met, first on the round-up and then, whenever he found an excuse to head into the city. Or days like today, helping their mutual friends. Her spunky, no-nonsense attitude appealed to him, except when she directed it *at* him.

21

Sam's sarcastic wit could be cutting at times, but he felt it to be a safety net of sorts, keeping her from becoming too serious in her relationships, especially with him.

He sighed and pushed back from the desk. What had happened to make her so prickly? He hated to think what she'd suffered in losing her arm, but was there more to it? Did she feel less of a person because of the prosthesis? No, not Sam. She'd stubbornly learned to use her left hand to maintain her independence. It had to be something else? But what?

Maybe he'd have the chance to ask Zakia on Saturday. He hated to go behind Sam's back, yet he needed to know and Zakia knew her better than anyone. Sam was certain to be at the cookout though, so he doubted he'd catch Zakia alone. His spirits lifted at the thought of seeing Sam again until he reminded himself that he would keep his distance. He resolutely pushed thoughts of her aside and went back to his paperwork.

* * * *

Friday morning arrived with a sense of expectancy that Sam fought hard to ignore. She left Brogan in charge of the shop and made a trip to the hardware store, arming herself with paint, rollers and brushes. When the shop closed at five o'clock, she locked up and cleared everything out of the way, ready for painting. That accomplished, she applied the first coat of paint, constantly watching the clock and wondering where Blake was. Maybe he'd had to check in with the Calgary police, or perhaps something happened in Fort McLeod to delay him.

While the initial coat dried, she ordered in a Chinese dinner for two, certain that he'd show up soon. She'd worked up quite an appetite since noon and, as it was nearing eight o'clock, she decided to eat without him. He could always nuke his when he arrived.

She applied the second coat of sage green to the walls and painted the counter and trim a contrasting forest green. By midnight, she'd cleaned the painting paraphernalia and put everything away. Blake hadn't showed or called and, dejected, she went up to her apartment, showered, and crawled into bed.

Why on Earth had she purchased a Queen-sized bed? It was too big for one person, and she'd never intended to share it. Or did she? Had she subconsciously hoped to develop some kind of relationship when she purchased it? Maybe a temporary one? Yeah, that's it! She needed a fuck buddy. She giggled, her mind automatically conjuring an image of her and Blake in that big bed. Yep, Blake would fit that role perfectly.

How many times in the past weeks had he turned her on with the briefest of looks or a casual touch? When he reached for her hand and grabbed the wrong one, he didn't shy away from her prosthesis, instead, he acted as if it was entirely normal to hold that hand. His devilish smile lit up his eyes, the smoky blue turning to the clearest sapphire. It warmed her heart to see him so happy and carefree. If only she could match his jest for life.

What if they did get together? It didn't have to involve commitment. What would his reaction be to her nakedness? The plastic surgeon had cleverly closed the stub of her severed arm by performing skin grafts, and tried valiantly to lessen the rest of the scars, but they were ugly. She hated to look at herself in a mirror, and she cringed when imagining Blake's reaction.

Then again, as a cop he'd probably seen many ghastly things. Maybe her scars wouldn't faze him a bit. Or maybe they could "do it" in the dark? She turned on her side, hugging the spare pillow and wondered why, on the one night he hadn't shown, was she thinking such thoughts? Not that she hadn't fantasized about him before, she had, but she'd always pushed such thoughts away. Well, except for that one time when she'd been so worked up and had to scratch that wanton itch herself.

She stared out the window at the moon where it hovered in the night sky. Was he lying awake thinking of her, or had she finally pushed him too far? Tomorrow— she'd see him tomorrow at the ranch. She'd drop a few hints, feel him out on it. She giggled again at the pun and, still smiling, dozed off, thinking about feeling a certain part of his anatomy.

* * * *

Up at daybreak, Blake fought the urge to drive into Calgary, much as he'd done the night before. Sam had really gotten under his skin. He missed her, felt a terrible ache where his heart should be, and it had only been a couple of days. He refilled his coffee cup and stepped out on the back verandah, never tiring of the view.

He'd built the ranch house on a knoll overlooking Clear Lake. Today the calm water resembled a mirror image, with the huge evergreens on the opposite side reflected in its surface.

His spread wasn't nearly as large as The Thunder Creek, but he was proud of his acreage just the same. He'd sunk all his earnings and plenty of hard work into making The Clear Lake Horse Ranch profitable. Raising horses involved plenty of skill, stamina, and patience.

The ranch provided riding lessons and wilderness adventure camps during which prospective buyers could try out their chosen horse and make certain it was a good fit for their needs. If he or any of his men witnessed an animal being mistreated or handled by force, he turned down the sale. Blake loved horses. In his mind, they deserved gentle handling and respect.

He'd hoped to bring Sam out here someday, and maybe he would, but right now he needed a little breathing space. At least here, her memory didn't haunt him so much. Once she'd ridden one of his horses or eaten at his table, he'd forever see her image superimposed over everything she touched. No, he wasn't ready to bring her here yet.

He set his empty cup on the outside table and crossed to the stables. He'd saddle up, go for a ride to clear the cobwebs from another sleepless night, and enjoy the peace of early morning on the range.

He tried to ride a different horse every day, although his foreman and ranch hands did an excellent job of exercising them daily. Today, he wanted Jet. The frisky, black stallion would love a brisk run and help keep his mind from straying to the memory of a curvy, dark-haired woman. It worked well until he stood at the edge of the lake, surveying his surroundings and remembering.

They'd gone dancing after dinner one night. When she spoke, her voice traveled through him like fine wine over an experienced palette. Sweet, bubbly, and tempting him to indulge in more than a brief taste, which was all she would allow. And when she moved, graceful as a panther, his libido went on red alert, daring him to ignore the vision now making an appearance in every dream and fantasy, asleep or awake.

Damn! He mounted up and rode back to the ranch yard, stabled his horse and brushed him down. He might as well head over to Luke's place. Maybe he could be of some use. And maybe, just maybe, Sam would arrive early.

* * * *

Awakened by the rattling and banging on the shop door, Sam crawled out of bed and crossed to the window.

Brrr! Mornings were sure getting chilly. She'd have to remember to close the window from now on.

"Who's there?" she hollered.

"Brogan," came the answer. "I forgot my key."

"I'll be down in a minute." Sam looked at the clock and groaned. She never overslept...never. She stepped over the pile of paint-spattered clothes from the evening before, pulled a clean T-shirt over her head and grabbed a pair of jeans. Barefoot, she descended to the main floor and unlocked the door.

"Wow! A bit of paint sure brightened this place up," Brogan said.

"Thanks. I got tired of the institutional gray," she replied, glancing around to see if she'd missed any spots. "I guess I should've started with the ceiling. It looks pretty drab now."

"Yeah, but who walks in and looks up? All our customers do is drop off and pick up their laundry."

"True, but it will bother me now. I'll pick up some flat white and do it tomorrow."

"Geesh, Sam! Don't you have a life?"

"Yep, and it involves you closing up today. I'm going to shower and get dressed then I'm outta here. You okay with that?" she asked.

"Sure." He grinned. "I love being Bossman and lording it over the hired hands."

Sam laughed. "Then I'm glad to oblige, but take it easy on the girls. They know their jobs."

"Yeah, I know. And being in charge is good practice for when I open my own business."

"Oh, what type of business?"

"Dry cleaning and laundry. This is what I know and I like it, you know, interacting with the customers, helping them out and all."

"Some of the messes that have come through those doors almost sent me screaming when I first opened. At least you know what you're letting yourself in for."

"Yep! So, where are you off to today? The ranch?"

She nodded. "They're having their last cookout of the year. Should be a blast. Zak said Luke even hired a band."

"Then git! And have a good time."

"Thanks, Brogan. See you on Monday."

By the time she'd cleaned the apartment, showered, and dressed, it was almost noon. She purchased the ceiling paint, stopped at a drive-thru for coffee and a bite to eat then headed her vehicle in the direction of the ranch. Oldies rock blared from the stereo and she found herself singing along to "Joy to the World" by Three Dog Night, although she received her share of odd looks before she cleared city limits. Sam smiled to herself. She didn't care what people thought. It was a gorgeous day, and she felt happy and carefree for the first time in weeks. Or was that anticipation? She had to admit, the thought of seeing one handsome cowboy in particular had her adrenaline running into overdrive.

She'd turned off on Route 519 when a sudden thud, then a thwack, thwack, thwack had her pulling over to park at the side of the road. *Damn! A flat!* She climbed out and went to look. Sure enough, the front tire on the passenger side picked up a nail. She could see the head of it shining in the sun.

Past experience told her the one thing a prosthesis wasn't any good for was trying to use a four-way wheel wrench. She dug into her jeans pocket for her cell phone. It wasn't there. *It must be in the truck.* She opened the side door and checked. Nope! What good was CAA if you couldn't call them for help? Hopefully, someone would come along and give her a hand.

Oops! She laughed. *Another pun. Getting good at this.* Thinking she might as well make good use of her time, she took down the spare tire, opened the back hatch, and retrieved the jack and wheel wrench. She jacked up the truck and blocked the rear wheels with a couple of large rocks, then waited. Her coffee had gone cold, but she drank it anyway. At least it was wet and quenched her thirst somewhat.

A good half hour went by before she heard a vehicle coming down the road. Ugh! Just her luck. After protesting and insisting she didn't need his help, who shows up but Blake. Prepared to eat a little crow, she smiled and walked over to his passenger window.

"Hi, Blake."

"Hi, Sam. Flat tire?"

"Yeah, picked up a nail."

"Rotten luck, but it looks like you have things well under control. I'll see you at the ranch."

He checked for traffic and moved to put the truck in gear. Sam panicked.

"Wait! No! I need your help."

"What?" He looked at her strangely as if he couldn't believe his ears.

"I can't turn the wheel wrench. Everything else is ready, but if I can't turn the damned wrench, I can't change the tire."

"Oh, of course. I forgot."

He shut off the truck and climbed down from the cab. "Glad to help." He smiled and went to the front of her truck and, with a few easy turns, had the wheel off and the spare mounted. After lowering the truck, he tightened the lug nuts and helped put everything away. "I noticed the CAA sticker on your side window. Why didn't you call them?"

She kicked some loose pebbles around with her foot and, still looking at the ground, replied. "I…uh…forgot my cell phone."

Blake laughed a full-bodied, deep from the belly laugh of genuine amusement. "Then it's a good thing I happened along. Luke sent me out for more paper plates. He has quite a crowd there already. It seems everyone wants to welcome Zakia home."

"Good. I'm glad she and Luke worked everything out."

"Yeah, it's nice to see them together again, speaking of which, I should get going."

"I'm right behind you," she said as he headed for his truck. "And Blake?"

"Yeah?"

"Thanks." She jumped in behind the wheel of her Chevy and headed to the ranch.

* * * *

Blake stood watching as she got in her truck and took off. That woman never ceased to amaze him. Seemed she really didn't like asking for help but could be somewhat gracious when the need arose. He smiled. So much for avoiding her and keeping his distance. At least he'd proved that she needed him sometimes. It felt good, real good. He climbed into his truck and continued on to the ranch, whistling a little ditty he'd heard the cowboys sing.

His good humor soon fled when he pulled into the ranch yard and saw Sam already surrounded by half a dozen wranglers. Apparently, Zakia wasn't the only one being made welcome. Perhaps now wasn't the best time to keep his distance. She needed someone to protect her from the roving hands and charming ways of those cowboys.

Huh! Who was he kidding? She'd done fine at putting him off. She could hold her own. Darned woman hadn't even glanced his way when he pulled in, and she had to know it was him. He spied Luke setting up tables near the fire pit and walked over.

"Here are the plates you wanted. Need a hand?"

"Sure do. I seem to have lost my helpers," he said, nodding in Sam's direction. "How come you're not over there?"

"Three's a crowd; six is a menagerie. I'll wait."

Luke laughed. "Then grab an end and help me get these tables set up. The food's almost ready."

Once that was done, the women put them to work hauling out trays heavily laden with food of every kind. Cook reigned over both fire pits, beef turning on one, pork on the other.

Lucas Senior supervised the construction of an outdoor dance floor, with a raised dais for the band and lights strung all around.

"Looks like it's going to be quite a shindig this year," said Blake.

"Yeah, Zakia wanted dancing so we'll dance."

"What's with all the tents?" Blake asked as he pointed to the area in front of the bunkhouse.

"The cookout is geared up a little different this year, what with the dancing and open bar. You know I don't take kindly to drinking and driving, so I informed everyone that if they're drinking, they stay put. Most of the neighbors brought tents, but there are a few RV's and campers parked behind the house as well."

"Good thinking. Makes my job a lot easier," said Blake, grinning in response.

"And eases my mind considerably. I don't want to be responsible for any accidents."

"I hear ya," Blake said, amazed at the sheer number of people present. "Any idea how many are here already?"

"Nope, lost count after Dad and his wranglers showed up, but it doesn't matter. Should be a good party."

"Yeah, it should be that," Blake answered, his eyes searching the crowd for a head of midnight black hair. "I wonder where Sam got off to."

"I saw her heading for the house a while back. Probably went in to talk to Zakia."

"Oh, okay. What's next on the agenda?"

"We eat."

"Sounds good. I've worked up an appetite." And it wasn't only for food. He watched Sam as she exited the back door and sauntered toward them balancing a tray of condiments on her good arm. She'd clipped her hair back today instead of drawing it back in a tight ponytail. A few stray tendrils curled toward her face, adding to her femininity. A long-sleeved, curve-hugging T-shirt outlined her ample breasts, and he sat, mesmerized, enjoying watching them bounce as she walked.

"Stop drooling, Blake," Luke said.

His mind snapped back to his surroundings. "I'm not drooling, but she sure is worth a second look."

"You've got it bad, my friend."

"What I've got is a permanent hard-on whenever that woman's around."

Luke guffawed and clapped him on the back. "Maybe it's time to do something about that."

"Hmmm, maybe." Unable to help himself, he walked over, relieved her of the tray, and set it down at the end of the first table. Surprised that she'd allowed him that tiny gesture, he asked, "Is there anything else to come outside? Those trays are heavy."

"Yeah, a couple more. They're not so much heavy as awkward for me." She smiled.

"Why don't you distribute this load among the tables while I go fetch the rest."

"Okay, thanks, Blake."

As soon as they had everything set up, Luke rang a cowbell to signal that dinner was ready. They served the multitude of children first and got them settled, then the adults lined up, took a plate and served themselves. Cook was in his element as he sliced beef and pork to top off their plates.

Blake and Sam joined Luke and his family where they sat beneath a maple tree.

"It turned out to be a beautiful day, Luke. What would you have done if it rained?" asked Sam.

"We cleaned out the big barn, just in case, but this is much better."

"Yes, it is. When will the band arrive?"

"They're here already," said Luke. "Now that the dance floor is finished, they can set up their equipment, but I told them to have dinner first."

"What's the name of the band?" she asked.

Luke laughed. "I'm not sure they've decided on one. They're a group of locals who come together to play at community functions. Some of the ranch hands will probably join them for a number or two. Do you sing?"

"I used to, not so much these days," she said, smiling.

"Maybe we can coax you onto the stage," Luke said.

Blake frowned at the suggestion. The men had ogled Sam all afternoon. He didn't think his nerves could stand to see her on display like that.

"You know, that sounds like fun. We'll see," she said.

"Blake usually joins in for a tune or two. Maybe you could go up together," said Luke.

"Sounds like a plan," said Blake, feeling better already at his friend's not-so-subtle matchmaking. "What songs do you know?"

For the first time in days, they were having a pleasant conversation and Blake rejoiced at how easily they decided on a couple of songs. It seemed their tastes in music were similar. He smiled, thinking about how many things they did have in common—mutual lust for one.

"I'm going for dessert. Anyone want anything?" asked Sam.

"Yeah," said Blake in a tone so low only she could hear. "But you won't find it on the table."

She laughed, the innuendo not lost on her. "Play your cards right and I might let you have a dance or two," she said before sashaying over to the table full of sweets.

Blake watched her go, admiring how the skintight jeans outlined her curvy tush. He wanted more than a dance or two. Maybe Luke was right. Tonight he'd make his move and see where it led. He was all done being a gentleman, waiting patiently for her to invite the intimacy he craved. If she turned him away again, well, he didn't know what he'd do.

He'd never believed in love at first sight—until he'd met Sam. And he'd walked around with a perpetual hard-on ever since. What did she feel? Did she become as turned on as he did when they were together? She was one hell of a sexy woman. Passion lurked below the surface. He'd felt it; felt the simmering heat of desire the few times she'd been in his arms. Could he stoke the flames until they ignited? Or was he imagining her reaction because he needed her? He couldn't imagine what had happened to make her turn cold at the slightest advance, but he was going to find out…tonight.

Chapter Three

The band set up right after dinner, starting with a rousing medley of country tunes that had adults and children both competing for space on the dance floor. Sam watched in amusement as the twins zeroed in on the same little girl. They might be young, but those boys knew what they liked. They took turns dancing, if you could call it that, with their pretty, dark-haired friend until they were almost asleep on their feet, and Luke announced that it was time for all the little ones to go to bed.

He'd had two huge tents set up near the house, one for boys and one for the girls. On this night, the twins would sleep there, with a couple of the older siblings keeping watch over the children in each tent. Sam was certain the older ones would entertain the children with ghost stories and the like until all had settled down for the night.

Blake came to sit beside her, drinks in hand.

"Enjoying the party?" he asked.

"Yes. There's certainly a good turn-out."

The band struck up a waltz to slow things down and he rose to his feet, holding out a hand. She knew that being held in his arms was dangerous, but without a doubt, it would be delightful, too. She took his hand and allowed him to lead her to the makeshift dance floor.

Dancing with Blake had every one of her hormones on full alert. His moves were sure and masterful, leading her around with no trouble to follow his steps. She felt as if she glided on air, her feet barely touching the floor.

When the next song proved even slower, he held her so close she could feel every beat of his heart as it thundered in her ear. Blake was a good head taller than she was, her cheek coming to rest against his chest as they danced. All her life she'd hated being short, until she'd found the perfect fit in Blake's arms. With him, she felt petite and cherished.

She became aware of his hardened length pressed against her belly and her nipples beaded in response. It had been such a long, long time since she'd been intimate with a man. Fear of seeing the disgust, or worse, pity, in their eyes when they looked upon her naked body for the first time, had kept her celibate since her accident. In truth, until meeting Blake, her desire had lain dormant, like a closed door to her very soul.

Now, she was all woman, with a woman's wants and needs the like of which she'd never experienced. Her awakening was due to the man holding her gently yet firmly against his heart. Maybe it was time to start living again—to feel the flush of heated skin against skin as they succumbed to their attraction for each other. He was interested. She knew that. Had known since that first day on the ranch when they'd all arrived to help Luke protect his wife, Zakia, from a crazed stalker.

"Sam?" His husky baritone sounded in her ear.

"Yes?"

"The dance is over." He chuckled. "Intermission. As much as I enjoy holding you, maybe we could sit for a spell?"

"Oh! Okay." She'd been so lost in thought, she hadn't been aware of anything except Blake's body against hers. "Want me to walk in front?" she teased.

He grinned. "Please do. Being this close to you has an obvious effect on my libido."

"Yeah, I noticed," she said, allowing her hand to trail down over the ridge in his jeans as she turned to start walking back to their table.

"Tease!"

She laughed and led the way, knowing his gaze stayed glued to her ass with every step. The heat of that stare caused a warmth deep inside, and her pussy gushed without warning. *Oh my stars! That has never happened to me before.*

She sat, feeling conspicuous with her damp panties, the unmistakable scent of her sex wafting upwards.

Blake leaned closer, his nose sniffing the air around her. "What's that scent you're wearing?"

"It's called In Heat. Do you like?" she replied, casting a smile in his direction.

"Oh yeah. I like. And are you?" he asked. "'In Heat'?"

"What do you think, cowboy?" She brazenly rested her hand on his upper thigh, close but not close enough to touch his hardness.

"I think…" he began as his eyes locked with hers. "I think you're quite a tease."

"Who says I'm teasing? I enjoy a good romp now and then."

"Then maybe we should adjourn to someplace more private."

She hesitated. Need vying with the urge to stay and party with her friends.

"I'm supposed to be crashing here for the night."

"We could slip away for a while and come back later."

"I thought we were going to sing together," she said, stalling while she made up her mind. She hated to confuse a good friendship with sex, but this man was so hot, her insides ached for him.

"Lady, I'll have your body humming to a fine tune in no time."

"Mmm, maybe we could go for a walk down by the creek?"

"Nope, too many people around. For what I have in mind, it's best not to be disturbed."

Those few words made up her mind for her. "Your place or mine?"

"Mine's closer."

"Should we say goodbye?"

Blake looked around. "There's no sign of Luke or Zakia. In this crowd, it could take all night to find them. Let's just go."

He took her hand and led her to his truck, opened the door, and helped her inside. She didn't protest. When he climbed in behind the wheel, he surprised her by hauling her close to his side and keeping an arm firmly wrapped around her as he drove. She didn't protest that either. It felt right—so gloriously right.

When he turned off onto another side road, she sat up straight and looked around. "Where are we going?"

"To my place."

"I thought you lived in Fort MacLeod."

"Nope, built a house overlooking Clear Lake a few years back." He glanced her way and smiled. "I may work in the city, but I'm a country boy at heart."

"Hey, I'm not complaining. I kind of like seeing you in tight Levi's and cowboy boots."

"Is that a fact?"

"Umm, hmm," she said as she cuddled against him once more. "You have a mighty fine ass, Northrup."

He laughed and hugged her tighter, a light squeeze. "Well now, ma'am, I'm kinda partial to yours, too. What they do to a pair of jeans should be illegal."

She felt red heat creep into her cheeks–a blush. She was blushing. She never blushed! It had been several years since she'd lost her shy innocence. The army took that out of a person in a hurry. What was it with this man? He made her feel different, act different: out of character somehow. Or was this her true self re-emerging? Was it time to put the past aside, bury the bittersweet memories in order to start living again?

Time would tell. She resolved to enjoy the evening and the man beside her. Tomorrow would come, whether she was ready for it or not. For now, it was enough that she'd taken this step. Her insides churned with anticipation and her pussy tingled, thinking of the night to come.

A nervous dread poured through her, making her feel slightly nauseous. What if her scars turned him off? Her body might fill out a pair of jeans all right, but she'd die of embarrassment if her scarred body held disgust for him. What if he turned away? Couldn't stand to look at her? To touch her? Hold her?

No, Blake was a better man than that. Wasn't he?
* * * *

Blake slowed the truck and turned into his driveway. He rounded the final turn before his house came into view and glanced sideways to witness Sam's reaction. He wasn't disappointed.

Her jaw dropped when the truck's high beams swept over the front of the building, spotlighting the two-storied Cape Cod with its wraparound verandah. The surface of the lake beyond shimmered in the moonlight.

"This is yours?" she asked, her voice full of wonder and her expression more animated than he'd ever seen as she turned to him.

He nodded, remaining silent.

"It's beautiful, Blake! However did you find such a perfect spot?"

"One of the quirks of my job." He smiled. "We had an escaped convict hiding out in the woods near here a few years back. The K-9 Unit tracked him down eventually, but I stumbled across this clearing during the search."

"Your own little piece of Paradise. I envy you," she said. Her voice hushed, almost reverent. "All I have is my cramped quarters above the shop."

He parked the truck and stepped down from the cab, held out his hand to assist her down then led her up the flagstone path to the front entrance. Just that morning he'd been certain he wouldn't bring her here, to his home, but as he unlocked the door and allowed her to precede him into the foyer, a sense of rightness overcame him. She belonged here…with him. All he had to do was convince her of that.

His cowboy boots sounded loud in the stillness of the night, the heels click-clicking as he crossed the ceramic-tiled floor. "Would you like a drink?" he asked, heading to the bar for some Dutch courage. She was here! His ardor hadn't cooled one iota, but he didn't want to move too fast for fear of her wanting to bolt, calling a premature end to the evening.

"Yes, but nothing too potent, thanks."

She stood in front of the room's huge glass windows, amazed at the perfection of the mirrored surface of the lake as it reflected the full moon.

"Oh! I bet that's a killer view during the daytime."

"Yes, and a calming one in the evenings, especially after a rough day."

She turned to look at him, understanding evident in her expression. "I imagine some worse than others."

"Yes, and I never quite get used to how horrid some people can be to the ones they profess to love. Enough of that. What'll you have? Beer or wine?"

"I'll stick with beer. I don't have much of a head for mixing my drinks."

She smiled a radiant smile as she accepted the proffered bottle.

That smile had his guts churning and his cock twitching in two seconds flat. Their fingers brushed, and he felt that simple touch all the way to his toes. Did she feel it, too?

Play it cool, Northrup. Take it easy!

"Would you like to sit in here or out on the verandah?"

"Oh, the verandah sounds lovely."

He flipped the latch and opened the door to a cool breeze blowing in off the lake. They crossed to the swing in mutual agreement, sat, and listened to the hushed silence as they sipped their drinks. Ever so cautious, he slipped his free arm around her shoulders and drew her into his embrace. The gentle rocking motion of the swing set a calm, relaxing mood at complete odds with the excitement and anticipation he felt churning through him.

"Are you warm enough?"

"Um, hmm," she murmured, snuggling in closer. "This is nice."

His chest swelled with pride. "What's nice is having you here to share it with. It gets pretty lonely at times." He hadn't meant to mention that last bit. The thought just snuck out of nowhere. Funny how he'd never felt the loneliness before.

"Much better than hearing traffic noise day and night."

"Yes, I appreciate that aspect of living out here, but it is nice having company too. Thank you for coming with me."

"Thank you for bringing me. It's a lovely spot."

She lifted her face toward him, and he couldn't hold back any longer. He wanted, no needed, to taste her. His lips brushed hers, tentatively at first, testing her reaction, then captured hers with a smoldering passion that seemed to fuse them together. He couldn't get enough. His tongue pushed against her teeth and she opened to him. Their tongues danced a duel of such tortuous pleasure, he groaned and tightened his hold on her.

Her arm came around his neck and her fingers threaded through his hair as she kissed him back. She matched his ardor with the tip of her tongue, thrust for thrust as they imitated the act this led them toward.

He eased back and taking her hand, rose to pull her up beside him. Without a word, they entered the house, pausing only for a moment as he locked the door then moved toward the stairs. At the bottom, he took her in his arms for one more breath-stealing, heart-pounding kiss.

"Are you sure this is what you want, Sam?" he asked as he searched her eyes for the truth. "If this has to stop, I need to know now."

She nodded and smiled up at him. "I'm sure. I just...."

"Just what?"

"I just hope sex doesn't muddy the waters of our friendship. You know I don't do commitment."

"We'll take it one step at a time. Who knows? Maybe sex between us will be so earth-shattering, we won't be able to keep our hands off each other."

"Maybe, but I'm glad you understand."

For now, he'd take what she was willing to give. He took her back into his arms and breathed a sigh of relief, hugging her tight before leading her up to his room. There was no need for artificial light as the moon shone bright through the skylight, spotlighting his king-sized bed in a way he'd never realized before. Seeing it, as if for the first time, he knew the time was right, the scene romantically set for making love to the beautiful woman at his side.

He'd never brought a woman home before and was at a loss as to what to do next. They stood there watching each other, like teenagers about to do the dirty for the first time, until she closed the distance. He smiled. That was his Sam. Once she made up her mind, she didn't hesitate to act on it.

As she neared, his arms opened wide to enclose her in a swift embrace. Her fingers pulled at the fabric of his shirt until the snaps released and she pushed it off his shoulders. He reached for the hem of her T-shirt, ready to pull it up and off over her head, but she stilled his movements.

"Just a sec." She undid the clip for the prosthesis and pulled it off, laying it on the dresser beside them. "Proceed."

He chuckled, taking up where he left off, and soon had her upper body bared to his view. His hungry eyes devoured the sight of her gorgeous breasts, their plumpness threatening to spill out over the top of her lacy bra. "Lady, that's one mean set of titties," he said before swooping down to cup their fullness, bringing one rosy peak to his mouth. She tasted like the purest of honeys. He suckled one and then the other, her soft moans egging him on. He wanted to please her – give her pleasure such as she had never known.

Her hand fumbled with his belt, and he reached down to undo it himself, gratified when she immediately loosed the snap on his jeans and lowered the zipper to take him in hand. Cool fingers did nothing to cool his longing for this long-legged beauty as she began to work his cock. Her fingers slid up and down the length of him until he thought he'd go mad with want.

He cupped her mound through her jeans, pleased at the dampness he found there as he rubbed back and forth, his other hand now undoing her jeans. Soon, they'd shoved the rest of the clothing to the floor, and he lifted her in his arms to lay her gently on the bed, before lying beside her.

The moonbeams cast a silvery glow to her features, her midnight black hair seeming to shine with a silvery aura. "You are so beautiful," he said as he smoothed the hair back from her face. He leaned forward, planting an array of kisses across her forehead, her nose, and then finding her mouth again. One arm slid beneath her, and he hugged her closer, content to let his other hand roam at will. He loved the feel of her, the satiny texture of her skin, and the silky smooth length of her hair as his fingers sifted through it to caress the nape of her neck.

All too soon, it wasn't enough. He worked his way down her body, stopping en route to suckle and knead her breasts until she squirmed beneath him in glorious abandon. Whatever inhibitions had kept her pushing him away were gone, lost in a sensuous sea, and he hoped they'd never return.

When he went lower and reached to spread her thighs, she surprised him by swinging one leg over his shoulders, opening herself up to him in a way he had dreamed of night after night. He dove into the warm, moist heat like a man searching for liquid in the driest of deserts. He laved and suckled her clit, rejoicing in her pleas for more. When the first orgasm came, he lapped up every drop. Then, and only then, did he rise to reach into the nightstand drawer and retrieve a small foil packet.

"Let me," she said, as she climbed to her knees beside him.

She ripped off the package with her teeth and spit it out then took her time rolling the condom on over the tip and smoothed it down his length.

Oh, sweet torture!

He lay back on the bed as she ministered to him, fondling his cock and balls until he was rock hard and ready to burst. When she straddled him, enclosing him in her wet heat, he almost exploded. He held her still for a moment, taking deep breaths to calm his raging libido then he moved. She matched his upward thrusts to her downward movements, riding his cock as if it was second nature, as if they'd been together like this before. No hesitation, no timid shyness. She wanted this joining as much as he needed it–needed her.

He rolled her over and thrust harder, faster, deeper. His hands reached to massage her breasts, and she arched her back to accommodate him. Her insides tightened, squeezing the head of his cock, and he knew she was close to a climax. He leaned forward and captured her mouth in a demanding, passionate kiss. She pulled him tighter, wound her legs around his hips and ground her pelvis against him in an effort to assuage her need as he pounded her pussy time and time again. When the dam burst, he collapsed in a heap by her side. He smiled. He could've sworn he saw stars.

* * * *

She couldn't find the words to say what she was feeling. No experience had ever compared to this. Sam cried, silent, happy tears, wiping them away with a corner of the blanket she'd pulled over their nude bodies.

"Sam, are you all right?"

She must have missed a teardrop or made some kind of sound to alert him. She could only nod against his chest.

He tilted her face up to his concerned gaze. "Then why are you crying? Did I hurt you?"

"No."

"Then what?"

"I'm so happy, it hurts."

He chuckled and hugged her closer. "Happy tears I can cope with. I'm feeling pretty good myself."

"It's never been like this for me."

"Like this, how?"

"Wonderful! Absolutely wonderful!"

"So, no regrets?"

"Not a one. You've made me feel alive again. I don't know how to thank you for that."

"No thanks necessary, but if you need to talk, I'm a pretty good listener."

She considered his words for a moment. Maybe if she shared her burdens with this caring, gentle man, the demons of her past would go away. Maybe they wouldn't haunt her memories anymore or cause endless sleepless nights.

"You sure you want to hear all the gory details?"

"Only if you're ready to share them with me."

"I warn you, it's not a pretty story."

"Most of what makes us who we are isn't pretty. At least in my line of work. I imagine your deployment to active duty wasn't all peaches and cream—not in a war-ravaged country."

"Not by a long shot." She took a deep breath, nodded her head, and began. "When I was stationed overseas, I met a man. A gorgeous man. He was a doctor there, and I'd helped transport some of our wounded to the clinic he'd set up."

It helped not having to see his face as she related her tale. The steady beat of his heart beneath her cheek calming her as the memories surfaced.

"I stayed and helped tend to the patients. All I had was a first aid course, but it came in handy that day. After twelve long, non-stop hours, everyone had been seen to and he asked me to accompany him to dinner. I went. We talked–had a lot in common, as it turned out. We ended up in bed that night and spent as much time together as we could over the next several months.

Our tour of duty was coming to an end. I was six months pregnant by then, working most of my days in the clinic. We looked forward to coming back to the US, getting married, and raising our child together."

Tears streamed down her face and her gut clenched, unable for the moment to continue. Blake just held her, his silent strength giving her the impetus she needed.

"Until the day the enemy shot down one of our helicopters bringing in more wounded. It all happened so fast. One minute, we were at the edge of the landing strip awaiting casualties; the next, we were casualties ourselves. Pieces of fiery, flying debris and molten hot metal rained from the sky. Doc took a piece to his chest and died en route to the clinic although I didn't know that until much later. The same piece of molten metal that sliced off my arm embedded itself in my stomach…in my baby, my unborn Clarissa."

"Oh, Sam! How awful!" He hugged her tight, his embrace comforting, soothing as she sobbed her heart out. "I wish you hadn't had to endure that kind of suffering."

"When I awoke and found out all that I'd lost, I wanted to die, too. They put me on suicide watch, gave me a medical discharge, and sent me home just as soon as

I was well enough. Then began many months of physical and psychotherapy until I was healed. Until I could put it all behind me and start living again. Except it wasn't really living. I didn't have a family, and I'd shut myself off from everybody else, except Zakia. Meeting her is probably what saved my sanity."

"Then I'm glad you managed to connect with her. Doubly glad, since your friendship enabled us to meet. At least now I can understand why you kept holding back for so long." He kissed the top of her head, his breath warm while her entire body had turned cold.

"It wasn't easy." She smiled, wiping away the last of her tears. "You're a persistent devil and handsome to boot."

"Ahhh! She thinks I'm handsome." He smirked.

"Don't let it go to your head. There are a lot of handsome men in this area."

"Yes, but you're not attracted to any of them or you wouldn't be here with me."

"True. I can't fault your logic on that score."

"I'm glad you're here and that you trust me enough to share your loss with me."

His hands were gentle, caressing, as he brushed stray tendrils of hair away from her face, his eyes locking with hers before straying to her lips. There was no time to reply as his mouth caught hers in a passionate kiss of tenderness and longing. He made her feel so special, so alive, so wanton as her body stirred to life again.

He took his time exploring her body, searching out the scars and kissing every raised bubble and ridge of skin. Her experience with the doctor was always a frenzied coupling, never knowing when the next casualties would arrive. No time for the tender foreplay that Blake excelled at. For the first time since her accident, she was honestly happy to be alive.

Chapter Four

Their return to Luke and Zakia's ranch was much later than planned, and Sam felt self-conscious as they pulled into the ranch yard.

"Do you think anyone noticed our absence?" she asked.

"Nah! The party's still in full swing. Hard to find anybody in this crowd," he said as he scanned the area. "Why? Are you worried about what people might think?"

She hesitated for a moment, thinking, wondering what she did feel. "No, I guess I'm not–not really."

"Then let's go join the others and show them how to have a good time."

He stepped down from the cab and held out his hand. She took it and shimmied under the wheel, surprised when he grabbed her around the waist and lifted her to the ground.

"Oh!" she said as her body slid down the length of him. "Maybe we should've stayed at your place." She allowed her body to rub against his, feeling the bulge in his pants.

"Oh, yeah! Too late now. We've been spotted."

They turned as one to see Zakia headed their way.

"Hey, you two! Glad you made it back. We've been waiting on you to sing for us."

"Damn!" Sam said as she slapped her forehead. "I totally forgot."

Zakia giggled. "That's all right. You're here now so, how about it?"

"Okay by me. Sam?"

"Yep. Lead me to the stage."

They sang a medley of country tunes that had the whole crowd dancing, clapping, and stomping their feet. Then they slowed it down to sing "I'm Your Lady" a song made famous by Canadian singer, Celine Dion.

Sam put heart and soul into the tune and felt that Blake did, too. The dancing slowed and the crowd hushed as the words spilled into the suddenly quiet night. When the song ended, Blake tugged her close for a quick kiss, then kept his arm around her as he said, "Good night, folks," into the microphone and led her off-stage.

"Wow! You guys were really good up there," Luke said.

"You had everybody so tuned in, the place rocked," said Zakia.

Sam felt heat rise in her cheeks and was thankful for the dim lighting. "Thanks! I enjoyed myself."

"I could tell," said Zakia, laughing good-naturedly.

"So did I," said Blake, hugging Sam close to his side. "But if you don't mind, I think we'll take off."

"Making decisions for me again, Blake?" Sam asked as she pulled slightly away from him.

"Yep! Any complaints?"

"Not this time." She smiled. "Good night Luke, Zak. I had a great time. Thanks for the invite."

Blake walked her to her Chevy Tracker. "I can always drive you over to pick it up tomorrow."

"Nope. I like having my own wheels. I'll follow you."

He swooped in for a heated kiss then let her go to open the door. "See that you do."

"Afraid I'll lose my way?"

"No. I'm more afraid you might cut and run."

She reached up to plant a kiss of her own on his hot lips. "Not on your life, cowboy. I want to see the rest of your house tomorrow and picnic by the lake."

"Is that the only reason you're coming with me?" he asked, his tone unsure.

"No. I'm coming with you because there are still a few night hours ahead of us."

The interior light showed the dazzling smile on his face. "Then let's git!"

He ushered her inside, practically ran to his truck, and pulled out onto the road ahead of her. She smiled as she drove, certain that he kept watch in his rearview mirror all the way. She parked alongside his truck, and he was there to open her door in a flash.

"I need to grab my bag."

"Allow me," he said and reached into the passenger seat for the large green duffle, a relic of her army days.

This time, she led the way to the door and waited while he fitted his key in the lock. She brushed past him as she entered, kicked off her boots, and went straight for the stairs. When she didn't hear him behind her, she stopped and looked down. There he was, duffle in hand, standing in his sock feet, with his mouth agape as he watched her.

"Well, are you coming?" she asked.

The words seemed to jerk him out of his sudden stupor. He smiled. "Yes, ma'am!" Then he took the stairs two at a time to catch up. She giggled and ran up the last few steps, and entered his bedroom mere seconds before he did. He dropped her duffle inside the door and caught her in time to wrestle her onto the bed.

"God! What a woman! You don't hesitate one iota once you've made up your mind."

"Are you bragging or complaining?" she teased, looking up at him, ready for his kisses.

"No complaints here," he said, then kissed her.

The kiss was passionate and demanding, wringing a response from her body the moment their lips met. Hungry for more, she tugged at his shirt, freed the snaps and wound her arms around his bare torso. His skin was hot to the touch, as was hers. She was on fire, as if they hadn't already made love earlier.

They kissed and caressed until she burned to have him inside her.

"We have too many clothes on," she said as soon as their lips parted to take another breath.

He stood and pulled her up beside him, then carefully, almost reverently, reached inside her shirt, undid the clip on her arm and removed the prosthesis, laying it on the nightstand. As she stood in front of him, he undressed her, sliding her top up and freeing her breasts from her bra at the same time. He tugged it up and over her head, his mouth sampling her turgid nipples. His hands went to the snap and zip of her jeans. Slowly, and ever so patiently, he pushed them down and off, raining kisses on her skin as it became exposed to his view.

She was jelly. Her legs no longer wanted to hold her up. She remained upright only because he never let go. He swung her up in his arms and laid her on the bed. He wasted no time shucking his clothes before parting her legs and hovering at the entrance to her moist pussy.

Sam would never tire of looking at this man. He was beautiful. His muscled body lean and fit, his cock huge and hard—for her. She held her arm out to him and he leaned forward for her kiss. He eased his hardened length inside, driving her crazy with the waiting, the wanting. She shoved upwards, taking him fully inside. Her good arm grabbed the spindle on the headboard for added leverage as she repeatedly arched her pelvis upward to meet his thrusts.

His breaths came faster, as did hers. She felt his heartbeat, the staccato rhythm in tune with her own. His movements increased in tempo, faster and faster. Her insides tightened, her orgasm not far off.

"Open your eyes, Sam. I want to see your eyes when you come."

Her gaze locked with his as her body clenched around him, urging his own release. She saw his eyes darken and felt the hot juice of his release mingle with her own as they climaxed together in molten heat.

Felt his juices? Shit! They forgot to use a condom.

"Ah, damn!" he said as he pulled out, a concerned expression on his face. "Shit, Sam! I'm sorry."

"I forgot, too. It's not just your responsibility, you know."

"Well, I should've remembered. I've never forgotten before."

She giggled. "Does that mean I turn you on, Northrup? Make you lose control?" she asked to break the tension.

He nuzzled her neck as he lay down beside her. "You know you do."

This would be the perfect time to enlighten him, but she didn't want anything to interfere with their night of passion. "To put your mind at ease, I'm clean and…it's, uh, the wrong time." There! She wasn't exactly lying to him, but it wasn't the whole truth either.

"Aw, honey, that's a relief. I'd never want to hurt you by bestowing an unplanned pregnancy."

"Hurt me? No, I wouldn't consider it as hurting. I love kids."

"You'd want to have my baby?" he asked, his voice incredulous.

"I'd love to have *a* baby. Yours would do nicely."

"Gee, thanks. I think."

"The question is, would *you* want to be a father?" She knew she was playing with fire, but she had to know.

"Hell, yeah! This place is too big for one person."

"Well, anyway, we're safe."

Long-time self-protective instincts kicked in. She was already half in love with the man and headed for certain heartbreak. His exuberance spoke volumes. She'd known, by the size of his house alone, that he wanted to be a father, yet chances were she'd never be able to give him that. She'd enjoy the rest of the weekend, store up memories to tide her over, but then she'd back off, for his sake. The thought filled her with dread. If all she had was two days with him, she'd damned well make the best of it.

"Beat you to the shower," she challenged, rising from the bed to run nude into the ensuite bath. He wasn't far behind.

She adjusted the taps while he ferreted out towels, then they both stepped into the shower. The corner cubicle was bigger than most, but it was still a tight fit with Blake being such a big man. She allowed the warm water to sluice down over her naked form as she grabbed the bar of soap and washed his chest. Her hand soapy enough to dispense with the soap, she took his erection in hand, stroking up and down the length of his dick before moving to cup his balls, gently soaping and massaging them clean.

Blake squirted shower gel into the palm of his hand and rubbed her all over, paying particular attention to her breasts and between her legs. Her pussy tingled at the intimacy involved in allowing a man to wash her private parts. He turned her to face the wall and soaped her ass, causing a riot of sensation to run rampant through her entire body.

She gloried in the feeling of his cock as it slid up and down the crack of her ass. Would he? Could he? He was so huge! She bent forward, unconsciously offering her ass up for him to explore. One arm snaked around her to rub her pussy while the other hand played with her rear. She felt him insert a finger and the bottom dropped out of her stomach. The feeling was so different, so intense. When he replaced his finger with the head of his cock, she tensed.

"Relax, sweetheart. We'll take it slow. I won't hurt you."

She relaxed and felt him inch inside bit by bit, and she pushed back against him, taking his cock even deeper. Sweet heaven! Her nerve endings sang a thrilling tune as he rode her ass. Bending forward even more, she placed her hand on the floor, rewarded when his hands came to hold her hips in place, pulling her back against him with every thrust.

He fucked her from behind with all the skill and stamina of a wild stallion. The climax, when it came, encompassed her entire body. Thrill after thrill, the roaring waves of her orgasm held her in thrall. Then he reached around to finger her pussy, and she literally exploded.

Blake withdrew and held her upright as he washed and rinsed their bodies then turned off the water. He wrapped her in a huge bath sheet, dried her off, and carried her to bed, returning to towel himself dry before joining her.

It seemed the most natural thing in the world for him to take her in his arms, cradling her close to his heart as, exhausted, they slept.

* * * *

Dawn found Blake on the rear verandah, coffee in hand, as he watched the sun rise above the horizon. He loved this time of day. So still and refreshing, uncluttered by the demands he might have to face before day's end.

Officially, it was his weekend off, but he often ended up at the office for one reason or another. Hopefully, not today. Today he wanted to spend with the raven-haired beauty asleep in his bed. Waking with her cuddled close had filled his heart with hope. He wondered how she'd feel this morning. Would she regret coming home with him? Could he convince her that they had something special going on between them?

He'd show her the ranch, picnic by the lake as she'd mentioned the night before, and go horseback riding through the valley. The last thought gave him pause. Could she ride?

All during Luke's roundup, she'd ridden in the wagon. Was it by choice, wanting to protect her friend? Or was it because she'd never learned to ride?

A slight noise alerted him to her presence, and he turned to see her framed in the doorway. She was wearing his silk robe, a Christmas present from his sister: the royal blue a perfect foil for her dark hair and creamy complexion.

She stood awkwardly, seeming uncertain, sipping her coffee as she watched him above the rim.

"Good morning. Sleep well?" he asked as he walked toward her.

"Very well. I thought the lack of traffic noise would keep me awake but I slept like a baby. Why didn't you wake me?"

"You slept so sound, I doubt a bomb going off would've woken you."

She flinched.

"Shit, Sam! I'm sorry. Poor choice of words."

"It's all right. That all happened a long time ago. Don't mince your words for my benefit."

She smiled up at him, and the sun truly shone on his day.

"What would you like for breakfast?"

"Coffee and toast is fine. I'm not much of a cook."

"Well, I am and I'm hungry. Join me?"

"Sure. What are we having?"

"I've some leftover roast chicken in the fridge, and I make a mean omelette."

"A chicken omelette? I'm game."

They went back inside. She refilled their coffee and sat at the table while he rummaged through the fridge for ingredients. When the omelette was ready, he filled both plates and joined her at the table. "Need anything else? Milk? Juice?"

"No, this is fine. It looks and smells delicious."

"Thank you. Now dig in."

"Mmmm. I wish I could cook like this. Take out is great on occasion, but every day gets to be a bore, not to mention hard on the budget."

"Is that why you don't eat breakfast?"

She nodded. "Toast and coffee I can do, sometimes cold cereal and juice, but that's the extent of my culinary abilities."

"How about sandwiches? I thought we'd pack a lunch for later and picnic down by the lake."

"Yep, sandwiches haven't proved a problem as yet."

"Then eat up and I'll show you the rest of the house. Do you ride?"

"Ride? As in horses? You have horses? Yes, I can ride!"

Her excitement was clearly visible; the gleam in her amber eyes almost catching fire.

He chuckled. "Yes, as in horses. We'll saddle up and go for a ride through the valley if you're up for it."

"Oh, yes! I'd love that. I'll just see to the dishes first." She stood and gathered the dirty dishes.

"No need. I'll do them later."

"It's only fair. You cooked breakfast so I'll clean up."

"I do have a dishwasher. Just rinse them and load it while I put the food away and wipe up the counter."

"Okay."

A few minutes later, he took her hand and led her on a tour of the house. The downstairs had a formal dining room, a den cum office, the living room, and a half bath big enough to accommodate the washer and dryer. Upstairs, there were four bedrooms, the master and a guest room with en suite baths and another full bath between the rooms on the other side of the hall.

"Your house is lovely, Blake! What I wouldn't give to have this much room to move around in."

He smirked inwardly. If he had his way, she would–and soon.

She'd turned toward him as she spoke, and he couldn't resist. He took her in his arms and held her close. "How about a kiss good morning?"

"It's about time," she said as her arm snaked around his neck to pull his head down to hers.

She really was a tiny, little thing. He lifted her off her feet and kissed her, holding her body tight against him. His reaction was swift and, acting decisively, strode to the bedroom in two long strides then carried her over to the bed. Untying the belt, he smoothed the robe back off her shoulders and let it fall in a heap on the floor. For the first time, he saw hers scars—really saw them.

He fell to his knees and kissed every one. How she must have suffered. Lifting his head, his eyes locked with hers, and in their depths he saw…what? Anxiety? Shame?

"You are beautiful, Sam. Exquisite!"

"Oh, Blake! I thought they might turn you off. I was afraid…."

"Shhh! I'm sorry you had to experience such pain and loss, but you are beautiful to me, inside and out."

He stood then and lay with her on the bed, running his hand along her curves and pulling her close as he kissed her again. A tender kiss of promise, of passion, of love.

Love? Is that what he was feeling? He tossed the word around in his mind, suddenly sure. Yes, he loved her. He'd thought of nothing and no one but her since the day they'd met. Should he tell her? No, he'd show her instead.

His hand came up to cup her breast, rolling the nipple between his thumb and forefinger until it hardened and puckered. Then he paid the same attention to the other one. His lips skimmed her nose, her eyes, and her ears. He blew hot breaths along her neck and kissed his way down to her gorgeous tits, taking first one and then the other into his mouth to lave and suckle until her body writhed in pleasure.

He continued his foray down her body, kissing his way to her most tender spot. She was already hot and wet for him. His tongue flicked out and teased the nub before delving inside to taste her essence. She squirmed and reached to pull him up beside her, but instead, he eased her over onto her belly. He kissed her backside, caressing her ass cheeks and blowing hot breaths up her crack. With gentle care, he moved down to lave the backs of her knees then moved upwards again, rubbing and caressing her spine as he kissed his way to the nape of her neck.

He lay down on his back and urged her on top of him, letting her take control to do as she pleased. Instead of mounting him, she moved to take him in hand. Her mouth closed over the head of his cock, her firm grip working its length as she teased and sucked the tip. She took him inside her mouth, sucking greedily as she caressed his balls. Never had he been so on fire for a woman! Fearing he might explode, he pulled her on top of him again.

This time she lowered her body, encompassing his dick in her warm, wet heat. She leaned forward, bracing her hands on his chest, and it was only then that he realized she still wore her prosthesis. That she could partly balance her weight on it. Not wanting her to hurt herself, he held her hips in place, working her lower body up and down on his cock.

This time, he took his time, prolonged the loving until he felt her insides tighten in warning. He released her hips and grabbed her tits, pinching and squeezing until she screamed his name. He pumped up into her a few more times to release his load, then sated, drew her down to his chest and wrapped her in a gentle embrace.

Neither spoke for a long, long while. He thought she might have fallen asleep, but she lifted her head and gazed into his eyes.

"Thank you, Blake, for showing me what making love is all about."

"Anytime, Darlin'," he drawled in a fake western twang.

"Seriously, I never knew it could be like this."

"It only gets better with practice," he said, lifting his eyebrows in a lascivious manner.

She smiled. "I'd be happy to get in a little more practice, but I thought I'd be riding a horse, not you."

"Why not both?" he asked, chuckling at her quick wit. "I'm not one to complain."

"Then let's shower up and get dressed. I really do want to go riding."

"Your wish is my command, but you need to get off me first."

She pushed herself upright and climbed off the bed to head for the shower. Watching her go, his cock started to harden again. What the hell! They had all day to go riding.

COVERT MISSION: UNDERCOVER COP

Chapter Five

It was almost midday by the time Sam mounted Sprite, a gentle, white mare that Blake picked out for her. He'd given her a tour of the stables, and she was impressed. He had quite an operation going on here. Where did he find time to manage all this and work full time as a cop, too?

She'd always loved horses but had never owned one. She was overjoyed to find out he bred them. True to his word, they'd packed a picnic lunch and rode along the edge of the lake. She glanced his way, and her body reacted to the sight of him riding a huge bay stallion.

Horse and rider rode as one, each seeming a natural extension of the other, and both gorgeous males. Blake sat erect in the saddle, a firm yet easy hold on the reins. Today, he was all cowboy...jeans, snap shirt, cowboy boots, and Stetson.

There was no sign of his other persona, that of a Mountie, although he filled out that uniform quite well. She'd stopped by the station a few times on one pretext or another, just to see him in uniform. If she was honest with herself, she'd wanted to see him–period. He had to have seen right through her flimsy excuses. She'd never chased after a man in her life, but she found she couldn't stay away from Blake. He was way too handsome, too good a man to pass up.

But she'd have to, especially since she'd seen his house. No man built a house that big unless he intended to fill it with family–something she couldn't give him. Some of the sparkle went out of her day, and she determinedly pushed those thoughts aside. She would enjoy this time with him. Enjoy it and then say goodbye.

"Watch the low-hanging branches. We veer off here, down a side trail."

"I thought we were having lunch by the lake?" she questioned.

"Near it, but this spot is better. You'll see," he said as he smiled back at her, a distinct twinkle in his eyes.

"Lead the way."

They slowed their mounts to a walk as they entered the trail to ride through the forest. She followed him a fair distance and could hear the sound of rushing water ahead. They came upon a clearing, and she saw it. A wonderful fall of water cascading out over a rocky incline to pool below.

"Blake! This is gorgeous! Thank you for bringing me here."

They rode to the edge of the pool and reined the horses to a stop.

"Do we need to tie them to something," she asked.

"Nope. Just let the reins drop. They won't go far."

"Okay."

Blake helped her dismount, something that was difficult to achieve with any dignity when one-handed. "Thanks."

"No need to thank me. I've been wanting to feel you against me since we left the ranch yard."

His embrace tightened, and she knew he intended to kiss her. She lifted her face to his and their lips met, mated, and passion built anew.

"I can't seem to get enough of you. Have you bewitched me?"

"Of course! Didn't you see me wiggle my nose before we dismounted?"

He laughed and picked her up to swing her around in a circle. "You never cease to surprise me. Life sure wouldn't be boring with you around."

"Speaking of which, is the water too cold to go swimming?"

"Nope! It's some kind of natural hot spring. Cold to the touch at the waterfall, but warm in the pool. Go figure."

"Good!" She sat down to remove her boots.

"What are you doing?"

"Going swimming. Care to join me?"

"Hot damn!"

He jumped around on one foot trying to remove his boots and finally succeeded. She'd stripped bare and headed for the water by the time he reached for his belt buckle.

"Hey! Wait for me!" he called.

She stopped and turned, delighted to watch him strip. When his cock spilled out straight and hard, she almost drooled. He strode purposefully toward her, magnificent in his nudity. She held out her arms. He walked into them and rubbed his body against hers as they stood kissing in broad daylight. There was something so decadent about being together like this. She felt naughty, wanton. Breaking away, she grabbed his hand and ran to the water.

"Don't you have to…uh…remove your arm?" he asked.

"Nope! Can't swim without it."

She laughed and tugged him into the water where they splashed and played like children. Where they came together and made splendid, glorious love, the buoyancy of the water adding a sensual touch as it swirled over their heated skin.

Paradise! She'd found Paradise, here–in this place–in this man's arms.

Her heart clenched at the thought of walking away.

But walk she would…for his sake. His happiness mattered much more than her own.

* * * *

He couldn't stop grinning. This had to be the best day of his life. A beautiful spot, an alluring woman and the best sex he'd ever had. Even the weather had co-operated. It was wonderfully warm for this time of year. They'd allowed the sun to dry their bodies as they ate, then lay in the grass and made love again. He'd hated to dress and leave, but she insisted on seeing the rest of his property. But when he got her home….

Home–even the word sounded like music to his ears. He'd always referred to it as "the ranch" or "the house," never as home. A home is filled with love and laughter. Until Sam, his never had been. Could he convince her to stay? To share his life? Was it too soon to ask? Did the word commitment even reside in her vocabulary? They were good together. Surely, she could see that. Feel it. Couldn't she?

He'd give it another night. Prove to her how good life with him would be.

"Race you across the field," she said.

Her words jerked him out of his reverie. "You're on!"

They raced across the field, and he found himself falling behind just to watch her ride. She sure could sit a horse! Her hair drifted on the wind as she rode, flying out behind her like a silken, black scarf. He loved how uninhibited she was, no matter what they were doing, or where. His grin suddenly faded.

He loved her! *Loved* her! Loved *her*!

This wasn't a casual fling, a temporary arrangement. He wanted to spend the rest of his days with her. And nights. Oh, the nights! He loved discovering new things about her every time they were together. He even loved her sarcastic sense of humor. He was toast!

If she knew how he felt he wouldn't see her for dust. It had taken a long time to break through her barriers. He couldn't pour his heart out to her this soon. She'd bolt for sure.

He'd take it easy. One day, one weekend at a time. He'd win her over, of that he was certain. She was a feisty, independent little thing, and he'd have to figure out a way to calm his protective instincts, but it was doable. Had to be. He just needed to figure out how.

"I won!" she hollered as she slowed her horse at the edge of the field.

"So you did. I'll beat you next time."

A sad look crossed her features but was gone so fast, he might have imagined it.

"Maybe, if you can pull some of the lead out of your ass. What's wrong with that stallion of yours? Letting this gentle little filly beat him. He should hang his head in shame."

Blake chuckled. "Maybe we just let you win."

"Don't give me your bull, Northrup! I won fair and square."

"If you say so." God, he loved sparring with her. He was still grinning like an idiot. She was a sight to behold. Hair mussed, face flushed and eyes blazing. Kind of like she'd just had the best sex ever. His dick perked up at the thought. "Seen enough? We should head back."

"I don't think I'd ever see enough. It's all so beautiful out here, especially with the leaves changing color. Winter will be upon us all too soon and days like today will just be a memory."

"Winter is harsh around here. That's a given. Shall we walk the horses for a bit?"

"Sure, they probably need a slower pace after that run."

They rode side by side, talking about anything and everything as they rode home. Blake enjoyed finding out more about her life, her likes and dislikes. She hadn't had it easy, growing up in foster care and being shuffled from home to home. After her parents died, she'd withdrawn and hadn't spoken for the longest time. Then she had gone through a rebellious stage, getting into constant trouble.

"So, I joined the army to get away from it all, make new friends, a new life for myself, the whole nine yards. And you know how that ended."

"Yes, but you're doing good now. You own your own business and have made a good life for yourself against some pretty tough odds. I'm pleased for you and proud of you. Given the same circumstances, I don't think I would've fared nearly as well. I tip my hat to you, m'lady." He suited action to his words and her resulting smile dispelled the melancholy.

"I think that, no matter what we have in life, there's always something more, something just out of reach."

"That's called life. We live it the best we can." Looking ahead, he spied the roof of the ranch house. "Race you home."

She didn't answer but spurred her horse and raced quickly ahead. Pleased to see her smiling face when she glanced back, he raced to catch up, arriving neck and neck in the ranch yard. A tie. He'd let her have the glory today. There would be other days.

They led their horses into the stables and removed the saddles. He was about to call one of his men to brush

Sprite down when Sam surprised him by picking up the currycomb. She talked to the horse in a soothing voice as she worked. This was a side of Sam he'd never seen. A gentle, truly caring side.

"Where did you learn to care for a horse?"

"Summer camp. The government paid for us to go for two weeks every year. I always signed up for riding camp. I love horses and the freedom I feel when I'm riding. Lots more fun than crafts and games with people I didn't know or particularly like."

"I hear you. I've always loved horses. When I was a boy, I dreamed of owning a horse ranch one day and now I do."

"And a fine ranch it is. Thank you for today, Blake. I had a great time."

"The day's not over yet." He put down the brush and walked over to wrap his arms around her from behind. "I've loved having you here."

She turned in his arms to face him. "I've loved everything about being here."

She kissed him then, her lips scorching in their intensity.

"Come on. Let's go up to the house before one of the ranch hands walks in on us."

She giggled. "Wouldn't that be something? Well, since you've gotten me hot and horny again, and as I'm not into public displays, I guess I'd better walk you home."

"If anyone walked in here now, I *would* be on public display. A man can't hide the fact like a woman can."

Her hand rubbed against the bulge in his jeans. "No kidding."

Holding hands, they ran to the house. They didn't make it upstairs. His need was too great. Swinging her around to face him effectively slowed her forward momentum as she came up against his chest. He kissed her soundly, all the while dancing to his own tune as he sidled them into the living room and over to the sofa.

He sat, hauling her onto his lap without breaking the kiss. Their tongues mated; their hands caressed, bringing their bodies to a fever pitch of wanting. Half undressing each other in unbridled passion, she stood long enough to discard her jeans then undid his belt and zipper. Freed of his jeans and boxers, his cock burst forth and she straddled his lap, lowering her body over the tip as he slipped inside her moist wet heat.

Balanced on her knees as she was, her bountiful breasts bounced in his face, tantalizing him—but not for long. He suckled one and kneaded the other, pleased when she rode him in earnest. Harder, faster. She slowed to rotate her pelvis on his; then harder and faster again, her movements perfectly in rhythm with his upward thrusts.

He allowed her to set the pace, knowing her independent nature and suspecting that her need was as great as his own. She sped up and slowed, over and over, driving him crazy. Finally, he felt the tightening he'd been waiting for, felt the hot juices cascade along the length of his cock. Only then, did he pump up inside her and, with a few quick thrusts, spilled his load.

Still joined, he lay back on the sofa, pulling her on top of him.

"You are one sexy lady," he said when he could breathe again.

"And you are one sexy cowboy. What's for dinner? I'm hungry. Must be all the fresh air around here."

"Must be." He chuckled. "I'll rustle up something in a few." He wiggled around to get a little more comfortable, holding her next to his heart.

"Okay," she said as she snuggled closer.

They dozed off in each other's arms, content–for now.

* * * *

Sam woke up wedged between a hard, hot body and the scratchy upholstery on the sofa. She tried to pull herself up by grabbing hold of the seat back, but couldn't, at least not without waking Blake. He had one arm still wrapped around her and, as she stirred, he tightened his hold.

"Where do you think you're going?" he asked in that low, sexy baritone that sent shivers up her spine.

"Nature call. Give me a hand, would you?"

He laughed, and she joined in the laughter as the pun dawned on her. "Well, you know what I mean. Help me outta here."

"Glad to oblige, pretty lady," he said in a low drawl.

His hands traveled slow and sure to her waist, building heat everywhere they touched. He moved her slightly and rose to stand naked and magnificent in front of her. She licked her lips at the evidence of his arousal.

"Don't you ever get enough?" she quipped, taking his proffered hand and moving gracefully to stand beside him.

"Nope, apparently not."

"You're insatiable!"

"Um, hum. You've met your match. I haven't heard you complaining."

She smiled sassily up at him. "What can I say? It's all your fault. If you weren't so devilishly handsome, a girl might get some rest around here."

"Hey, we just rested for an hour. What more do you want?"

"Food!"

His low chuckle warmed her heart.

"Okay. Duty calls. It's off to the kitchen I go."

He began to walk in that direction.

"Hey! Aren't you forgetting something?"

When he turned back, she threw his jeans at him then ran for the bathroom, still stark naked.

She heard him chuckling all the way to the kitchen. When she emerged, she stopped long enough to pull his discarded T-shirt over her head. As she'd guessed, it covered her to mid-thigh. Delicious smells were already wafting from the kitchen, and her stomach growled a warning.

"There is something infinitely sexy about a nearly naked man cooking," she said as she padded barefoot across the floor. It was all she could do to keep her mind on her rumbling stomach and not ravish him there and then. Jeesh! Now she was the insatiable one! "What cha making?"

She waited anxiously for the moment when he glanced her way and saw what she was wearing. Would he be pleased, or would he be pissed?

He turned, looked her up and down, and whistled. Then he smiled a devilish smile and she knew it was okay.

"Spaghetti and ground beef. Sorry, no time for meatballs."

"With something smelling that good, I'm not one to complain."

"Good. I'd hate to have to withdraw my offer of sustenance because you were being ungrateful," he teased.

"Uh, uh, not me. I love home cooking. I just can't cook."

"Can you stick a couple slices of garlic bread in the microwave to reheat?"

"Sure. Only a couple?"

"Or three."

"Okay. That sounds better." She reached to give him a chaste kiss on the cheek, but he turned his head and theirs lips connected. That's all it took. She ached with need as his mouth plundered hers and she was almost ready to forgo nourishment…until her stomach growled again.

She grabbed the loaf of garlic bread, cut off a few good slices and nuked them. The flavor proved too tempting to an empty stomach and she munched on a chunk of it as he finished preparing dinner. "Want me to make coffee or something?"

"At this time of night? You want coffee?" He turned a surprised look her way, and she glanced at the wall clock.

"Yeah, kind of, but it's all right. I can do without." She knew her voice sounded petulant and she hated that, especially since he'd done so much for her today, but she did love her coffee. Sometimes, when in the army, that's all that kept them going through the long, sleepless nights.

"There's a jar of instant decaf in the cupboard. Will that do?"

"Sounds like heaven! You've a serious coffee-aholic here. As long as it smells like it, I'll drink it." She laughed and put the kettle on then headed to the cupboard he pointed out. "What'll you have?"

"I think I'll have a beer. It's in the fridge."

"Coming right up." She passed him the bottle and busied herself setting the table as he dished up their meal.

They ate in companionable silence, but every time their eyes met across the table, her insides zinged with anticipation.

"Can you stay another night or do you have to get back to the city?"

Another night? Yes! She wanted as much time as she could have with this man. He tilted her world in a way she doubted she'd ever recover from, but she wanted—no, needed, this time with him. Or so she convinced herself.

"Yes, I can stay, but I have to leave early for the hearing."

"Right, then let's leave the dishes and go for a walk. Or would you rather watch a movie?"

"How about a walk and then a movie?"

"Okay, but we'd better get dressed first. Wouldn't want to spook the horses."

She giggled. She seemed to do a lot of that around him. "Or your ranch hands."

"Right! They can find their own woman. Don't need them eyeing mine."

He wrapped an arm around her shoulders as they walked back to the front room. His words thrilled her soul and haunted her at the same time. If only she *could* be his woman.

Chapter Six

He led Sam to the back garden, their way dimly lit by solar lighting embedded along the path. Toward the far end of the garden was a pagoda, under which stood an old-fashioned garden swing. The four-seater was excellent for nights like tonight. A light breeze blew in from the lake, but the surrounding shrubbery protected them from the worst of it.

They sat and he pushed off, allowing the swing to rock them gently as they cuddled together on one side. "Are you warm enough?" She'd pulled a sweatshirt on over her T-shirt, but he didn't want her catching a chill.

"Toasty. Cuddling close to you is like cozying up next to a blast furnace. Your skin is always hot to the touch and it seeps right through that jacket you're wearing."

"I'm just hot for you," he said as he dropped a quick kiss on the top of her head. "Stick with me and you'll always be warm."

"Among other things," she teased.

"Ummm, interesting. Shall we go back inside and tend to those 'other things' then?"

"Can we just sit here for a while longer? It's so peaceful and quiet."

"Anything you want." He hugged her tighter, and they sat soaking up the restful calm of the night. Clouds hid the dim light of the moon and a fine mist of fog hovered overhead. "I think we're in for some rain."

"Maybe we'd better go inside. I only have one change of clothes left, and I need them for morning."

He kept his arm around her as they retraced their steps to the house. "Still want to watch a movie?"

"If it's all the same to you, I can think of better things to spend our time on," she said, an unholy grin spreading across her face as she glanced up at him.

"Lady, I love the way you think! Just let me lock up and I'll meet you upstairs."

"Okay."

When he arrived in his bedroom, he heard the shower running, but before he could join her, she'd turned off the water and he waited. She appeared wearing only a towel, sarong fashion, hiding her missing arm. Whew! What a hot, sexy woman she was. He crossed the room and took her in his arms for a deep, passionate kiss that had his toes curling in his boots and his cock standing at attention.

"I'll be right back," he said as he headed for the shower.

He took a long, cold shower to cool his ardor. Tonight he wanted to make slow, gentle love to her, if it was at all possible. She really stoked his fire! What a woman!

But when he returned to the bedroom, he found her sound asleep in his bed. Crawling in beside her, he pulled her close and gloried in the fact that she was there. Maybe he'd take the day off tomorrow and convince her to do the same. It had been one hell of a hot weekend, and he hated to see it end. Would she feel the same way?

He awoke to the feel of her warm breath teasing his nipple sometime during the night. She sucked it into her mouth and then blew on it, the hot-cold sensation gripping him in its intensity. His hard male nub hardened even farther. No wonder women enjoyed having their breasts toyed with. He'd always thought it akin to mimicking a nursing child, catering to their nurturing nature, but this was like nothing he'd ever experienced.

So intimate, so caring a gesture, and so much of a turn on.

His quick, indrawn breath must have alerted her to the fact that he was awake. She came up on her elbow and kissed him.

"Good morning."

"Is it morning? What a way to wake up." He glanced at the digital clock on the nightstand. Four thirty. Yep, technically, it was morning. He tugged her closer for another kiss, this one deeper, passion-filled, as desire zoomed through his system. A man could get used to this real quick. He loved waking up to this hot, willing woman in his bed.

He turned toward her, his erection pushing against her lower belly, and she struggled to reach it with her hand.

"Urgh! This isn't working! I need to feel you," she said as she repositioned herself. Her arm, severed just above the elbow, wouldn't support her for long, but she balanced on it in order to reach his cock. She gripped him with a firm hand then ran it up and down the length of him. He sucked in a breath at the first touch of her cold fingers.

"Your skin feels like silk stretched over steel, hard and soft at the same time," she said.

"Hard I can understand, especially with your attention focused on it. How could it be anything else?"

She looked at him and smiled. "Harder."

That was all she said, all the warning he received before her mouth covered his engorged dick. Her hot, wet mouth drove him insane with need. His hands clenched in her hair then let go to grab the bed sheet. Her tongue tickled the head of his cock as she sucked. The wanting, the waiting to be inside her, was pure torture, yet her ministrations made him feel so amazingly good. Enough!

He pulled her up beside him and half straddled her as he bent forward to suckle a turgid nipple. She arched into him and held his head tight against her. He took it as a signal to deepen his attentions, sucking harder, squeezing and nipping until she squirmed beneath him.

"Now, Blake. Take me now," she urged.

With one last, long tug, he released her nipple and rose above her, positioning his cock at the apex of her thighs. Her pussy moist and ready for him, he pushed inside with one huge thrust, delighted when she gasped his name aloud.

"Yes, Blake. Yes!"

He drove into her again, and she lifted her legs to wrap them around his hips. This time, his cock delved even deeper as he thrust inside her slick, wet warmth. He so wanted to take his time, to pleasure her, but control slipped away from him when they were together. She met him thrust for thrust and when he tried to slow down, to regain a semblance of control over his raging libido, she'd have none of it, pushing up and down on his cock even as he held himself still above her. What a woman! She knew what she wanted and was determined to get it. Release. His and hers.

His thrusts became harder, faster, deeper, bringing him to the brink of pleasure and pain as a dazzling climax overcame him. His seed spilled inside her, and he collapsed at her side, hauling her close. He dozed for a while, awaking only when the sun streamed in through the window. He looked at the woman nestled in his arms, the sun casting bluish streaks in her raven tresses. Beautiful!

"Wake up, sleepyhead. We have to get moving if you want breakfast before we leave." He kissed her forehead as she tilted her head toward his voice.

"Just a few more minutes," she said as she snuggled closer. "I don't want to move just yet."

"All right, but only a few." It was pure torture holding her naked body close and knowing they didn't have time for a repeat of their early morning loving. She stretched languidly beside him, one leg coming up to rest on his own and causing his cock to spring to attention.

"Woman, you're killing me here."

He was rewarded with her shy giggle as she rubbed her pussy against his leg. "You're asking for it," he warned.

"Um, hmm."

Up and over in a flash, he embedded his cock deep inside, pleased when she arched to meet him. Their coupling was hurried, but welcome. In a frenzy of need, they came together all too soon, but rose from the bed smiling and hit the shower.

Yep, he could sure get used to this.
* * * *

Blake followed Sam as she drove into Calgary. They arrived as the bailiff came to close the door. The courtroom packed to full capacity, Blake led Sam to a seat midway on the far isle and shuffled in beside her. They waited. He wondered what was going on. These proceedings normally started promptly at nine o'clock, and it was already nine twenty.

The bailiff went out a side door near the front of the room and the reporters present murmured among themselves. He saw Luke put a comforting arm around his wife, his mouth moving as he spoke to her in hushed tones.

When the bailiff reentered, his "All rise" signaled the entrance of the presiding Judge. A collective sigh of relief was short-lived as Judge Landers spoke.

"It is my understanding that Leroy Williams, who some of you know as Roy Grayson, escaped on the way to the courthouse today."

The crowd erupted with questions and the judge banged his gavel.

"Order in the court! Order in the court or I will clear the courtroom."

The room became silent again, so hushed you couldn't hear a single intake of breath.

"Now, in regard to this new development, my staff is arranging protective custody for the Manning family until Mr. Williams is apprehended."

Blake lifted his arm high and stood. When the judge nodded permission, he spoke. "Your Honor, I am Constable Blake Northrup of the RCMP detachment in Fort MacLeod. With your permission, my staff and I are ready and willing to provide protection for the Manning family."

"Mr. Manning, I understand Williams broke through your defenses once before. A safe house might be better at this point, but it's your choice. Are you agreeable to Constable Northrup's offer?"

Luke and Lucas Sr. stood to address the judge. "Yes, Your Honor. We are."

"Then Constable Northrup, I leave them in your capable hands. Court adjourned." He banged his gavel and all in attendance rose to their feet as he departed the courtroom. The reporters were the first out the door. This was news in the making.

Blake and Sam made their way over to Luke and his family. Luke had Zakia wrapped protectively in his arms, and both seemed to have taken the news rather well.

"Rotten luck, Luke. I'll check into it and find out what happened. First, we need to get you guys safely home."

"Send a patrol car out to the ranch. Pete's there with the boys, but I'd like added protection until we get there."

"You've got it, Luke! I also need to contact the Calgary Detachment to enlist an additional escort for the drive back."

"DuShane is here somewhere. I'll call the ranch and alert Pete while you check with him about the escort. That bastard's not getting through this time." Winnie flinched, and Luke rushed into speech again. "I'm sorry, Winnie. I know he's your son, but my main priority right now is protecting my family. That includes you and Dad."

"Roy wouldn't hurt me," she said in protest. "I wish they would've allowed me to speak with him. This whole thing doesn't make any sense. Why would he even try to escape?"

"Sorry again, but running only proves his guilt," said Luke. "He could be miles away by now, but I'm not taking any chances. We'll hole up together at Thunder Creek. It'll be easier for Blake and his men to guard us that way and less disruption for the children."

"I'll arrange for Brogan to watch the shop and move in with you guys for the time being, if you have the room."

"No problem," said Zakia, a weak smile on her face. "I'll feel safer with you along."

"Fat lot of good I did last time!"

"Sam, that wasn't your fault. Hopefully, this time he doesn't have access to more tranquilizer darts," said Luke.

"Amen to that. Okay, I'm off. I'll make arrangements for the shop, pack some clean clothes and see you back at the ranch later."

Blake listened intently to the conversation as he arranged for a second vehicle with Officer DuShane. He hated to see her go without one last hug or a kiss, but now was not the time or the place. He waved in her direction and she waved back, smiling as she went on her way. His heart lightened considerably knowing she'd be at the ranch. He'd see her again later today. Right now, he had a job to do.

A few moments later, Sam came rushing back in and ran up to him.

"Blake! It's like a circus out there—reporters and television crews, all waiting to record Zakia's reaction to the escape. I could barely push the door open. Where do they all come from?"

"I was afraid of this. It's all right, Sam. Thanks for the warning. We'll take them out the back. Can you get to your truck?"

"Not without a lot of pushing and shoving."

"Then I'll walk you out the back. You okay with that, DuShane?"

"No problem. I'll hold the fort."

"Thanks. Be right back." He admired Sam for her feisty, independent nature, but was happy to help her out when she needed it—something that didn't happen often enough.

He placed a hand in the middle of her back as he guided her out of the room and into a hallway. A couple of turns later, they were alone…totally alone. He swung her into his arms for an arousing, tongue-dueling kiss.

"I've been wanting to do that since court adjourned."

"What stopped you?" she said as she slid her arms around his waist.

"Not the right time or place. So, you'll be at the ranch later? Luke's ranch?"

"Uh, huh."

"Good! Maybe we'll manage a few stolen moments."

"Ah, Blake, we're going there to protect our friends, not to continue our weekend rendezvous."

"Why can't we do both?"

"He got Zak once before. I'm not going to let that happen this time."

"Neither am I," he stated rather forcefully. "Am I'm the one in charge of guard duty."

"You were the last time, too."

He held her away from him, looked into her eyes, trying to see the truth there. "So what are you saying? You think I'm incompetent?"

"No, I'm saying we need to have our priorities straight and concentrate on the job, not our sexual prowess."

More than slightly miffed at her trying to tell him how to do his job, he pulled away. "Speaking of which, I need to get back." He pointed toward the end of the hall. "That's the outside door. Can you make it to your vehicle from here?"

"Of course!" She stepped back, then turned and walked away.

Sashayed, more like. She wore skin tight, black jeans that outlined every curve with each step. Combined with high heeled, hooker type boots, she oozed sex appeal. He watched until she disappeared out the door and allowed it to slam shut in the quiet hall, never once looking back.

He'd been sharper than he'd intended. He knew that, but who did she think she was trying to tell him how to do his job? Cops were allowed to have a life, too. Shaking his head in resignation, he resolved to straighten her out on that fact later, then returned to the courtroom and the duties that awaited him.

* * * *

In the end, they had two additional escorts. Blake led the procession in his Dodge Ram, followed by Luke and Zakia in her Caddy, then a patrol car, Lucas and Winnie in her bright red Mustang, then DuShane in an unmarked police cruiser.

One of DuShane's men sat beside him in the truck, his eyes constantly scanning the road ahead, as were Blake's, although his mind kept wandering. It's a good thing he had DuShane's man along as a look-out. He had a hard enough time concentrating on his driving; images of sexy Samantha kept popping into his mind.

DuShane brought up the rear of the procession. He'd brought a couple of his men with him to watch for anything suspicious. He'd also assigned a guard to drive Luke's and Lucas Senior's vehicles, while they sat in the back with their wives.

The two other patrol cars would see them safely to Thunder Creek then continue on to the Grayson ranch. They'd stand guard while Lucas informed his foreman of their temporary change of address and Winnie packed. Blake had radioed ahead for a team of his men to check both properties.

So far, so good. Of course, this was the main highway. If Roy and his cronies intended an ambush of any kind, he'd do it on the forested side road to the ranch or at the Thunder Creek itself. He needed to be alert, but damned if his thoughts didn't stray towards Sam more often than not. He'd intended to convince Sam to give them a chance, but Roy's escape and their subsequent argument put a severe dent into that plan.

While they'd waited at the courthouse for back-up to arrive, DuShane filled them in on the escape. The Sheriff's van had turned a corner to find a transport blocking the road, forcing their vehicle to a stop. Witnesses in a nearby coffee shop said the men in the Sheriff's van hadn't even had a chance to radio for assistance. Masked men appeared out of nowhere and bullets peppered the windshield, killing the driver and guard. Roy and his cellmate were set free and rushed down a side street by the masked men.

The whole episode stunk as far as Blake was concerned. Who was Roy working with that they'd kill to release him? Or was it to aid the other prisoner's escape? If so, why would they drag Roy along with them? Why not kill him, too? No, Roy had to be in on it somehow.

Too many questions swirled around in his brain. Blake's job was to guard the Mannings, not figure out the who and why of things, but one persistent question remained–just who were those masked men?

* * * *

Why did men have to have such prickly egos? All she did was try to cool it with him while they had to protect their friends. She'd cooled it all right. Maybe it was for the best. There wasn't a future in sight for them anyway.

Sam parked in the alley behind the shop and entered her building through the back door to scoot upstairs for a quick shower and change of clothes. She threw a load of wash into the machine and repacked her duffle bag in preparation for an extended stay at Thunder Creek. She cleaned the apartment and sorted through the fridge items that wouldn't keep, and packed them in an insulated bag to take with her. The washing machine shut off so she switched her clean clothes to the dryer and went down to the shop.

Brogan was at the counter serving one of her regular customers when she appeared, so she made small talk for a moment then busied herself with paperwork until Brogan was free.

"Hey, Boss! How did the hearing go?"

"It didn't. Williams escaped on the way there."

"Really? That totally sucks!" He stood with hands on hips, oozing attitude from every pore. "How did he manage that?"

"Yep, sucks a big one. I don't have the foggiest idea how he managed it, but he did. I'm heading out to the ranch for an extended stay until they capture the louse and put him behind bars again. Are you all right running things here? Any problems I should know about?"

"No problems." He grinned. "I'm happy to run the place in your absence. Do I get a raise or a new title or something? Assistant Manager sounds real nice." His pretty boy face wreathed in smiles as he stood waiting for her answer.

He really was quite attractive. Her customers loved him. She laughed, as he'd meant her to. "Yep, you can have the title. As to the raise…let's wait and see if we end this month in the black."

"Fair enough. How long do you think you'll be gone?"

"I have no idea, but I'll keep my cell on in case you need me."

"That's good to know, but we'll be fine here. You concentrate on helping your friend."

"Thanks, Brogan. I'll be leaving in about an hour, just waiting on some clothes to dry."

"Need help with anything?"

"Nope! Everything's under control."

"Yeah, and I should know better than to ask by now."

Had she really been that hard to get along with? She smiled. "Yes, you should, but thanks for the offer. See you later."

After losing her arm and everything else the way she did, the road to recovery hadn't come easy. Maybe she'd leaned too hard on the self-sufficiency angle in her determination to be independent. She snorted aloud on her way back upstairs. There was no maybe about it. She'd become the Queen of Independence...except with Blake this past weekend.

Simply thinking about her cowboy cop had her insides quivering with remembered rapture. He sure knew how to make a woman feel alive. In his arms she'd felt whole again, complete. The prosthesis, her horrid scars – nothing seemed to faze him enough to turn away.

Perhaps it would've been better if they had. A future together was impossible. He deserved better than what she could give him. Blake was a nice man, a gentle man, and sexy as all get out. Her mind went to mush as she pictured him standing tall and erect, magnificent in his nudity. That man was really hot! Scorching hot! She'd carry his imprint for days to come. No doubt about it.

Excited at the prospect of spending more time with him, she was also afraid of their friends regarding them as a couple. That would make the break so much harder when it came.

The buzzer on the dryer signaled the end of the cycle, interrupting her thoughts. She folded her clothes and finished packing by rote, her mind still fixated on Blake.

They'd had such a glorious weekend together. Everything had been so perfect...the man, the sex, the house, the cooking, the horseback riding, and the shared communication. She'd allowed herself one weekend of bliss, two days in which to store up memories. Was fate lending a hand in throwing them together again? They'd be in close proximity over the coming days–maybe even weeks–and that fact had her heart racing, pounding heavily within her chest.

Would she be able to ignore her attraction to him in order to protect her friend? Could they manage a few stolen moments here and there? Or should she avoid him in the hopes that he'd think it was only a spur of the moment fling on her part?

No, after all the time he'd spent pursuing her, he wouldn't believe that for a moment. She sighed as she closed the duffle, no closer to a solution than she'd been earlier. She'd have to wait and see how things went at the ranch. With a little luck, they'd catch Williams and she could go back to living her life her way. Only, that prospect didn't have the same appeal as it had before Blake.

She thumbed her cell phone open and called the ranch. "Hi, Zak! You got home okay?"

"Good!"

"Yes, I had a few things to see to but I'm leaving here now. Need anything?"

"Okay then, see you soon." She pocketed the phone, grabbed her duffle and the bag of perishables and headed out.

Chapter Seven

"Blake, I'm worried about Sam. She should've been here by now," said Zakia as she prepared dinner.

She'd echoed his thoughts exactly. After overhearing their telephone conversation earlier, Blake had found himself constantly on the lookout, not for an escaped convict, but for Samantha's Chevy tracker. "Maybe she had to stop for gas or something."

"Even so, it shouldn't take her three hours to get here. And she's not answering her phone."

"I know. I'm beginning to worry, too. Perhaps she was held up at the shop, some kind of emergency." He tried to think positive, coherently. It wouldn't do anyone any good if he panicked. He'd wanted to call and check on her but she hadn't given him her cell number, and if everything *was* okay, she'd lambaste him for sure.

"She would have called. This is so not like her," Zakia said as she stopped peeling potatoes to glance his way.

"If it'll make you feel better, I'll call the station and see if there are any accident reports."

"Please do. We have to do something."

He went out the kitchen door onto the back deck and called in. A few fender benders in town due to black ice that morning, but nothing since. Deciding to act and not wait around any longer, he waved one of his men over.

"Jake, Sam was supposed to be here hours ago, and we haven't heard a word from her. I need to drive up toward Calgary and see if I can find her. Can you stay with Zakia and the boys until I return? Luke rode out with his men to check on some stock, but he should be back soon."

"No problem, Boss. Hope she's all right."

"Me too, Jake. Me, too." He went back inside followed by Jake.

"Zakia, Jake's going to stay in the house with you until I get back. Lucas and Winnie still watching TV with the twins?"

"Yes, find her, Blake. Take all the time you need. We'll be fine."

He tipped his hat in farewell and headed for the truck. His foot wanted to push down hard on the accelerator, but he was afraid he might miss something if he drove too fast. He scoured both sides of the road as he drove, more worried than he'd ever remembered being in his life,

What could have detained her? Why hadn't she called? Instinct told him she couldn't, and his instincts were usually bang on. If anything had happened to her, he didn't know what he'd do. She'd come to mean so much to him, and he hadn't even told her how he felt. Granted, he'd showed her in as many ways as he could, but the words hadn't been said.

Maybe she just didn't want to face him after the way they parted at the courthouse.

No, she wasn't the type to abandon her friend due to a petty misunderstanding with him. If she could have, she would've been at the ranch before now. Shoving personal thoughts aside, he concentrated on the here and now, constantly scanning for a glimpse of her Chevy. Even so, he almost missed it.

Alerted by the fresh skid marks, he slowed, and peered off to the side of the road where they led. There! He braked to a stop and jumped from the cab. Sam's tracker, painted up in camouflage green, rested on its driver's side in the dense undergrowth.

"Sam! Sam!" he yelled as he ran to the front of the vehicle. He caught a glimpse of her unmoving body through the busted windshield. "Sam, can you hear me?" he shouted. He peeled the broken glass away and pulled out a pocketknife to slice through the airbag blocking his view.

No answer. Her head rested against the driver's door, her features peaceful, as if asleep, or…. No! He reached in to feel for a pulse. It was weak but there. Thank, God! "I'll be right back, sweetheart. I need to call for an ambulance."

He ran to his truck and called it in, grabbed his first aid kit and hurried back to Sam. Blake crawled gingerly through the broken windshield and along the dashboard then crouched as close as possible to her still form to check for broken bones. Damn! Her good, left arm was swollen and bleeding. He couldn't tell if it was sprained or broken, and he didn't want to move her, but he had to stop the bleeding. He grabbed a tourniquet and tied it around her forearm, just above the elbow. After he'd pulled out a piece of broken mirror, he cleaned the cut as best he could, packed on some gauze pads and applied a wrap to keep them in place.

She had a nasty bump on the side of her head, which probably accounted for the concussion. "Come on, Sam. Wake up. Talk to me." He sat, holding her hand and talking to her until the paramedics arrived and ushered him out so they could take over.

It's no easy task to remove an unconscious person from an overturned vehicle, but they did it with a minimum of fuss. Blake hovered at the edge of the action, willing her to open her eyes and assure him she was all right. His prayers answered only moments before they loaded her into the ambulance, he rushed to her side.

"How do you feel? What happened? I'm so glad you're awake!"

She looked at him as if he'd sprouted horns. "I feel like shit. I don't know what *happened*. And who in the hell are you?"

Blake, happy to hear her no-nonsense tone, didn't register the final question for a moment. "Geesh, Sam! That knock on the head must've shaken your marbles. I'm Blake." At her blank stare, he continued, "Blake Northrup." He focused on her eyes for any flare of recognition. Nada. Zip. Nothing. "Constable Blake Northrup of the Royal Canadian Mounted Police."

She looked up at him as if seeing him for the first time, confusion etched on her features. "Should I know you? And…Sam…is that my name?" she asked.

His heart went out to her at the hell she must be going through if she didn't even know her own name. "Yes, it's short for Samantha."

"Sir, we need to get our patient to the hospital."

"Fort MacLeod Health Centre?"

"Yes, sir."

"I'll see you there." Then to Sam he said, "I need to wait here until the Forensics Team arrives, but I'll join you shortly."

"Why? I can't answer your questions."

He reached out a tentative hand, careful not to spook her, and caressed her cheek lovingly. "Sam, I need to be with you. Understand?"

She focused on his eyes and must have seen the answer she sought. "I think so."

Her eyes drifted closed again as they loaded the stretcher inside. He watched, torn, as the ambulance pulled away, sirens blaring and lights flashing. He wanted to be with her, but he had a job to do. Sam was an expert driver. Someone or something made her lose control. He needed to find out which.

First, he called Forensics then a tow truck and back-up. He grabbed his roll of yellow crime scene tape and cordoned off the area, reducing the country road to one lane, but it couldn't be helped. He measured the skid marks. Whatever had happened out here caused her to lock-up her brakes. How long ago? He sniffed the air for the scent of burning rubber. Nothing.

He crossed the ditch to take a better look at her truck. The back bumper, dented and mangled, caught his attention. Dark blue paint had transferred to Sam's vehicle. He returned to his truck and grabbed the mini forensics kit he kept there. Returning to Sam's vehicle, he used his pocketknife to scrape some of the blue paint into a zip lock baggie. It was obvious to Blake that Sam's little Chevy had been rammed from behind. With the force of the impact, some evidence may have fallen from the other vehicle.

Sam must have been scared out of her mind. Knowing her as he did, she wouldn't have panicked, but she would attempt to outrun or outmaneuver her followers. She probably tried to make a run for the ranch, knowing he and his men were already there.

Had she been knocked unconscious immediately upon impact? Or had that happened due to a loss of blood? The lump on her head would signify the former, but, if so, who had turned the key to shut down the truck's engine? Who had left her here to die?

Blake's hands fisted at his sides. A killing rage boiled up inside him. A rage such as he'd never known in all his years on the force. This case was different. It was personal. Whoever had been behind the wheel of the second vehicle had made a big mistake. He, or she, had messed with the woman he loved. He vowed there and then that justice would be his. He'd find the bastard responsible and make him pay!

He heard the approaching sirens and gathered up his equipment. He thought to grab Sam's duffle bag and threw it onto the passenger seat of his truck. She'd be thankful for a clean change of clothes. He then called Zakia to fill her in, but didn't mention his suspicions or Sam's amnesia. As soon as he'd briefed the arriving members of his team, he was out of there, en route to the hospital to see his beloved Samantha.

* * * *

Damn! It wasn't bad enough that doctors and nurses had poked and prodded her for the past hour, now she found out that her prosthesis had a busted finger. She'd have to order a new one. She drew a blank as to how she'd go about it. This amnesia crap was wearing on her nerves! Why couldn't she remember anything?

One of the nurses had kindly clipped it back in place after all the x-rays and tests were done, but it looked sad with the pinky broken.

An orderly came in and checked her wrist ID. "Hi, Sam. I have orders to wheel you down to the plaster room."

"Plaster?"

He tucked the blankets around her, unlocked the wheels of her stretcher and steered her out into the hall. "Yep. Sorry to be the one to tell you, but your left arm has a hairline fracture. You'll be wearing a cast for the next few weeks."

"Great! How am I supposed to wipe my ass?"

He laughed so loud at her outburst that everyone stared at them as they went by. "You do have two arms," he finally said.

"I do?" She hauled her other arm out from under the blanket.

"Ah, sorry about that. I guess it might be a problem after all."

Sam grinned at his discomfiture. That should teach him to laugh and poke fun at someone before he had all the facts.

The attendant in the plaster room was the total opposite. He was gentle and caring and oh so serious. The shot of Demerol they'd given her on arrival had kept the pain at bay, and the ice packs had reduced the swelling, but she hadn't prepared herself for the necessity of a cast. The man talked while he worked, the soft sound of his voice helping to calm her frayed nerves.

"I see your other arm took a hit as well. Perhaps I can fix that pinky for you. It would hold until you can arrange for another."

"Can you? That would be great!" She smiled as she watched him work. When he finished the cast on her arm, he splinted the broken finger and applied a layer of gauze.

"There! All better!" he pronounced.

"It certainly looks much better than a busted knuckle. Thank you."

"You're welcome. Take care."

The attendant rang for the orderly, and he whisked her back to her room. Blake sat in the single visitor's chair but rose to stand as they entered. Behind him was the most beautiful bouquet she'd ever seen. And that balloon! So funny! She tried not to laugh, but once she started, she couldn't stop. The laughter turned to tears, and she couldn't stop those either. She couldn't remember anyone ever bringing her flowers before. In fact, she couldn't remember anything – period.

* * * *

Blake rushed into the emergency unit as if the hounds of hell nipped at his heels, only to find out that Sam was in x-ray and he had to fill out her paperwork. That done, he went to the gift shop and purchased an enormous fruit basket filled with goodies. He picked out the biggest bouquet they had along with a brightly colored, helium-filled balloon. It sported a monkey in traction with the caption "Get Well Soon" emblazoned across both sides. He chuckled when he saw it, despite his worry, and hoped it would lift Sam's spirits as well.

He returned to her room, which was still empty, placed his purchases on the windowsill and sat down to wait. His stomach rumbled, and he glanced at his watch to see that it was way past dinnertime, and he hadn't eaten since Zakia had fixed sandwiches at noon. Thinking he'd go to the cafeteria and grab a bite, he looked up to see an orderly wheel Sam back into the room.

"Hey! How are you doing?" he asked as he stood to greet her.

"Just peachy! They give good drugs here."

The orderly chuckled on his way out.

Blake smiled at her attempt at humor, but he saw her arm in the cast and knew she must be in pain. "Careful now. You're talking to a cop, remember?"

"Yeah, that's about the only thing I remember. What was your name again?"

"Blake. What's the doc saying about your memory?"

"They think it's only temporary due to the accident. No lasting damage."

"Well, that's good news."

"Yeah, but this isn't," she said, glancing pointedly at the cast.

"It'll make things difficult for a while, but not surmountable."

"Spoken by a man with two good arms. Tell me, how am I supposed to attend to business? My right arm is virtually useless, and now my left is out of commission."

"We'll manage. You're not alone in this, you know."

She regarded him with a "who are you trying to kid" expression.

"Seriously, I'll help with…whatever needs doing." His mind conjured instant images of helping her dress and undress, feeding her, brushing her raven hair.

She snorted. "Yeah, I'm going to let a strange man wipe my arse. Forget it!"

"You got any better ideas?"

"Are we married or something? I'm not wearing a ring."

"No, we're not married, but we're close, real close."

"Fuck buddies?" she asked.

Her blunt language surprised him. "More than that, but our relationship is complicated."

"How complicated?"

"You're a stubborn, independent, career woman who made me chase and pester you until you gave in. We just spent our first weekend together."

"Gee! You make me sound adorable."

"You are." He grinned and sat on the edge of the bed.

"Make yourself comfortable."

"I intend to. Is there anything else you need to know?"

She seemed deep in thought for a moment before she looked straight at him and asked, "Who am I, Blake? What do I work at? What kind of accident put me here?"

"Your name is Samantha Muldoon. You're ex-military and run a dry cleaning shop in Calgary." He paused for a minute, wondering just how much to tell her, deciding on the truth. She needed to know that her life was in danger. "You were on your way to a friend's house when someone forced your vehicle off the road."

"Oh, wow! You don't sugarcoat anything, do you?"

"Not when your life hangs in the balance."

"Okay, I get that, but why do I have enemies? Who hates me enough to want me dead?"

"I wish I knew. Do you remember anything before the accident?"

"Not really, just brief flashes here and there. This friend, who is it?"

"Her name is Zakia Manning. She lives with her husband, Luke, and their twin boys on The Thunder Creek Ranch. Ring any bells?"

"Not a one. You said I was ex-military. Is that where I lost my arm?"

He felt now was not the time to tell her what else she'd lost, so he kept it simple. "Yes."

She relaxed against the pillows for the first time since coming into the room.

"You need rest. Maybe I should go."

"Do you have to? I mean…well, you're the only one who knows anything about me. What if I have more questions?"

"You can't force the memories, Sam. When the trauma of what you've been through today wears off, they'll come back."

"Thank you, Dr. Northrup. Such sage advice. So, are you leaving or staying?"

"I'm staying right here. Get some sleep if you can." His words must have reassured her, for she dozed off almost immediately.

She was still sleeping when the doctor entered the room.

"How's our patient?" he asked.

"You tell me, doc. This amnesia, is it anything to worry about?"

"It's difficult to say at this point. She could wake up and remember everything, or this could go on for weeks."

"So, other than the broken arm, is she all right?" Blake asked, unable to keep the worry out of his voice.

"Some bad bruising and a nasty cut on her arm, but we sealed it before sending her for the cast. She's going to hurt for a few days, for sure."

"How soon before she can go home?"

"I'd like to admit her overnight for observation, but otherwise, she's good to go."

"Then get me some pants. I'm outta here," she said from the bed, startling both men.

"I recommend you stay the night. You were unconscious for quite a while and lost a lot of blood. I'd feel better if you stayed put," said the doctor.

"I'm fine. Just give me something for the pain and I'm good. Where are my clothes?"

"The clothes you wore on admittance the police bagged as evidence," said the doctor.

"Well, I'm not walking out of here in a Johnny shirt and having every Tom, Dick, and Harry ogling my ass."

Blake laughed at the picture she presented.

"I'm glad you find that amusing."

"Oh it is. It really is. Your duffle bag is in my truck. I'll go grab it while the doc here signs your walking papers. And don't worry, doc. I'll keep a close eye on her."

"Harumph!" came from the bed as both men left the room.

Blake grinned all the way to the truck. She might not remember anything, but she was still the same feisty, outspoken woman he'd fallen in love with. Maybe even a little more so. He'd never heard her use such graphic language before. Nursing her back to health would be a chore he'd relish, starting with dressing her to leave the hospital.

When he reached her room, she was sitting on the edge of the bed, her feet dangling above the footstool. She certainly didn't lack determination. Still, that had to be quite a feat with no hands, although she was in better physical shape than most.

He closed the door and pulled the curtain around the bed for extra privacy, then rummaged through her duffle for something easy to slip on over the cast. A button up shirt with long, puffy sleeves seemed to be just the thing.

"Blake, are you sure about this? I can call a nurse to help me dress."

He stepped in front of her and took her face in both hands then leaned in for a kiss. "Let me do this for you, sweetheart. I may be a stranger to you right now, but believe me, I've seen, kissed, and caressed every inch of your gorgeous body. I know you must feel scared and uncomfortable, but let me care for you. Okay?"

She nodded.

He untied the Johnny shirt and unsnapped the sleeves. It fell away to expose her breasts, so rounded and beautiful he wanted to touch, to taste. Instead, he picked up the shirt and eased it on over the cast, then helped slip the other arm inside.

"I'm sorry. Did you want a bra?"

She blushed and shook her head. "No, this is fine."

He eased her socks on over extremely cold feet then reached for her jeans. She put her feet in them, and he tugged them up to her knees then helped her to a standing position so he could pull them up. She swayed dangerously, and he held her close until she steadied. "All right now?"

"Yes, just a little weak and dizzy."

He loved the way she clung to him. As much as he hated to, he held her slightly away from him so she wouldn't be scared off by his reaction. His cock always sprang to life around her. That was nothing new to him, but in her current state…. "It might be a good idea for you to stay the night here."

"Trying to get rid of me already?"

She glanced up, her lips barely a hair's breadth from his.

"Not at all. I'm trying to think of what's best for you."

"Getting out of here is what's best. I hate hospitals!"

She spoke with such vehemence, it was clear she remembered. "Good! You're remembering already."

She smiled at him. "Yes, I am, aren't I?"

He wanted to kiss her so bad, his lips ached for it. Luckily, the nurse arrived with the wheelchair.

"Where are my boots?" Sam asked.

"Evidence, most likely," said Blake. "Don't worry. The nurse will wheel you down to the door, and then I'll carry you to the truck. You don't need boots for that."

"Just as well, since I don't seem to have a choice."

He smiled and helped her into the chair, zipped up her duffle and slung the strap over his shoulder, prepared to leave. It was really too bad about the amnesia, but he couldn't help preening at being able to care for her. She'd always shunned his protective instincts, but as long as she couldn't remember, he wouldn't enlighten her. The next few days would be interesting, to say the least. If only he could keep his libido in check.

Chapter Eight

Sam hated being dependent on anybody for anything. That much she *did* remember. Although having a sexy man kneel at her feet to put her stockings on sure sent an unbelievable thrill rocketing through her bruised and battered body. It certainly remembered his touch, even if she didn't.

When the Johnny shirt had fallen away and left her exposed to his view, she thought she'd die of embarrassment…until she witnessed desire flare to life in his eyes. That was when she knew everything would be all right. He'd take care of her until she could do so herself, whether she liked it or not.

The nurse waited at the hospital entrance with her while Blake went to bring his truck around. He swung her up in his arms as if she weighed next to nothing and lifted her into the passenger seat as promised, careful not to bash her damaged arm on the doorpost.

Her body reacted immediately to the close contact. Heat coursed through her veins–molten heat. Her nipples beaded, and her pussy twitched. It was almost a relief to sit in the truck while the nurse passed him her flowers and fruit basket. Until he leaned around her and she caught a whiff of his clean, manly scent. He smelled of the outdoors and sunshine. Her senses went into overdrive, and she almost reached up to pull him closer. Almost. Her prosthesis wasn't really co-operating since the accident. Something was wrong with the bend and reach mechanism. She'd have to find out where to order a replacement. Surely, she had paperwork on it at her place. Damn!

"Where do I live? Are you taking me home?"

"You live in an apartment above your dry cleaning shop, but right now we're headed to your friend Zakia's place."

"Why? Wouldn't it be easier to take me home?"

"No can do. I have a job there."

"You said she lives on a ranch, right?" He nodded. "What kind of work does a cop sign on for at a ranch?"

"Security. That's why you were going there as well."

She snorted and gulped back a harsh laugh. "Security work? What good would I be now with no arms? She probably doesn't need a piece of useless flesh hanging around to wait on."

"Don't kid yourself. Zakia will love having you. The two of you are best friends and you're not useless. With your military background, your instincts and observations are spot on. And you still have one…uh…good arm. You always seem to handle yourself well enough."

"Yeah, maybe, when it's working right. I need to have it replaced, but I don't remember how to go about it."

"There may be military records on that. I'll check into it for you. Your insurance should cover the replacement."

"Oh, I hope so. Thanks."

Blake turned left onto a side road.

"Does this lead to the ranch?"

"Yes. Why?"

"It seems familiar."

When they came upon the skid marks, she tensed. "Is this where I left the road?"

"Yes. If I hadn't been out searching for you, you might've been lost in those bushes for days."

"Why? Surely someone would have seen the skid marks and gone to investigate."

"Maybe, but your truck is painted up in green camouflage detail and blended in too good for an occasional glance from passersby to notice.'

"Oh. What kind of truck? Where is it?"

"A Chevy Tracker and I've had it impounded. Forensics is going over it with a fine-toothed comb. It rolled on its side, and someone shut off the engine. I don't think it was you, so we're checking for fingerprints and stuff."

"Was there much damage?"

"There didn't seem to be, but I was more focused on you. It had a broken windshield and bashed in bumper, but I was gone before the tow truck got here, so it's hard to say."

"You said I own my own business. Do I have any money? Enough to fix it?"

"I really don't know. You seem to do a good business, but we never talked about it much. As to fixing your truck, the insurance should cover that."

"Oh! Okay."

Made out of logs and rough-hewn lumber, the massive, elaborate archway with signage signified they were entering the Thunder Creek Ranch. None of it looked remotely familiar to Sam and her hopes of recovering her memory dimmed. "Have I been here before?"

"Yes, plenty of times."

"Why can't I remember?"

"Don't beat yourself up about it, Sam."

"Easy for you to say! You're not the one with a huge, gaping hole in your mind."

"No, but the doctor warned against trying too hard. Let it come naturally…and it will, Sam. Give it time."

The ranch house and yard came into view, and she sat straighter in her seat. The two-story house tugged at a memory then disappeared, as did the covered wagon parked beside the barn. Before the truck came to a halt at the front porch, a woman and two little boys appeared. Twin boys…boys that she knew! Tears filled her eyes as the loveable urchins climbed onto the running board to peer inside at her.

"Auntie Sam! Auntie Sam!" they chorused.

Blake pressed the button to roll down her window.

"Hi, Casey, Cammy," she said.

"You're crying!" said Cammy.

"Are you sad?" asked Casey.

"Nope, I'm just so happy to see you."

Blake reached to turn her head toward him, gently wiping the tears from her eyes. "See, I told you you'd remember."

Zakia ushered the boys down and opened the truck door, shooing them backwards to prevent them from climbing up again. "Sam, are you all right?"

She nodded her head, smiling as she spoke. "I am now, Zak. You and the boys are the first people I've recognized since I awoke."

"Good! That's a start. Now, how do we get you down from there without hurting you?"

"I'll take care of that." Blake stepped down from the truck and walked to the other side. She turned to face him. Placing his hands at her waist, he easily lifted her to the ground. "Okay?" he asked as he steadied her.

"Yeah, but don't let go. I'm still kind of weak at the knees."

"You got it." He kept his arm around her as they walked to the door.

Zakia and the boys led the way to the living room where a massive fireplace was blazing much-needed warmth. Sam had never felt so cold, at least, not that she could remember. She settled into a rocking chair beside the hearth and, sensing her need, Zakia spread a blanket over her lap.

"Would you like to have a pillow to support that arm?"

"Yes, please, if it's no bother."

"No bother at all." Zakia grabbed a big, fluffy one from the sofa and helped arrange it under her busted arm.

"Thanks, Zak. That helps take the strain off. This da–" She caught herself. "—darned cast is heavy."

Blake chuckled, his eyes lighting up with mirth at her choice of words, but no way would she curse in front of Zak's boys.

"Would you like a coffee or something to eat?" asked Zakia. "We've had our dinner but I saved some for you two."

"That sounds great! I'm starving!"

"Sam, you're always starving. I don't know how you stay so tiny," said Zakia, laughing. "I'll go heat up your plates and be right back."

"Wouldn't it be easier for you to sit at the table, Sam?" asked Blake.

"Oh, dear! I'm so sorry! I never even thought," said Zakia.

"That's okay, Zak. Yes, I'll come to the kitchen."

Balancing her uncooperative prosthetic elbow on the table enabled her to eat without much fuss, although she noticed that Zakia had been kind enough to cut up her steak for her. Picking up and drinking from her coffee mug proved more challenging, but after a few frustrating attempts, she managed it.

Through it all, she felt Blake watch her like a hawk does its prey. It was disconcerting, with her struggling to feed herself, but reassuring as well. If she needed help, he'd assist in a heartbeat.

After dinner, Blake surprised her with a sling to help support her broken arm.

"Thank you. Where did you find it?"

"I had one in my emergency kit that I'd brought in earlier today. Would you like to go for a walk?"

She was exhausted and hurting beyond belief, but one look in his serious, concern-filled eyes told her that he needed this. "Yes, I think I'd enjoy a walk."

Blake guided her out the back door and down the steps in the direction of the barn.

"We can't stray too far from the safety of the house and yard. Hard to say who's out there," he said as he scanned the surrounding area.

"So, I know I should've asked this before—who are we guarding and why?"

"We're here to guard Luke, Zakia, and the boys. A stalker followed her for months. You helped her leave town safely, and she ran to Luke. The stalker found them here. We eventually caught him, but he escaped custody on his way to the hearing this morning. So we're back on guard duty."

"Wow! This sure has been an eventful day for you."

"Yeah, I could've done without you getting hurt. I was so worried."

"You were?"

They'd stopped at the corral fence and turned toward each other. Sam could feel his intent before he lowered his head and kissed her, cautiously. It was a nice kiss, tasting of sweetened coffee. When she didn't protest, he held her closer and kissed her more thoroughly. So thoroughly, her knees weakened again and this time it wasn't from lack of blood.

"Is it always like this between us? So intense?"

"Oh, yeah. Right from the start, although we fought it as long as we could."

"Why?"

"Well, you always made it clear that you weren't into commitment. We went out several times, dining, dancing, movies, the museum, but you wouldn't even call them dates. They were outings. Friends being friendly. I hated being your 'friend' when I'd hoped for so much more."

"Then how did we end up in bed together?"

"I'm not sure. I don't know what happened to change your mind. We were here at Luke's year end barbeque last Saturday, and we ended up together."

"Here?" she asked, glancing around, wondering where they might have found some privacy. The barn maybe?

"No. As horny as you made me, I didn't lay you down in the nearest field. We went to my place."

"Oh! So it wasn't just a spontaneous coupling, then."

He chuckled, his breath blowing hot against her ear as he brushed her hair back off her face. "Spontaneous combustion if we hadn't gotten out of here in time."

She smiled. "I have no doubts as to being hot for you. You are one sexy cowboy. If my arm wasn't hurting so bad, I might want a repeat."

He stiffened immediately, pulling up to his full height. "I'm sorry. I forgot about your arm. Do you want to head back?"

"In a minute or two. What I'd like is for you to kiss me again."

This time he lifted her so she could rest her arms on his shoulders, held her close and kissed her possessively, passionately, sparking an answering fire deep in her breasts, her belly and lower. Moisture pooled at the juncture of her thighs. She was hot!

All too soon, he ended the kiss and lowered her to her feet. By mutual agreement, they walked back to the house, said their good nights and went upstairs. Blake had arranged to have a cot in his room. He'd sleep on it and be handy if she needed him.

"Blake, you don't have to sleep on that cot."

"Yes, I do. For one, I don't want to hurt your arm, and two, if I was in that bed with you, I wouldn't sleep at all for the wanting."

"Who says we have to sleep?" she asked.

"Sam, you don't even know me. You don't remember me at all. It would be like making love to a stranger."

"So? I've heard said somewhere that a change is as good as a rest. You said we'd spent the weekend together, so we're not strangers. I just need to feel that something is real."

He took her face in his hands, large, strong hands, and tilted her chin up so he could stare into her eyes. Then he kissed her again. "That's real. What we shared is real. But when we make love again, I want you to know who you're making love to. Until then, I sleep on the cot. Now, let me find your pajamas."

He helped her wash up and dress for bed, tucked her in, and turned out the light.

"Thanks, Blake."

"No problem. Sleep well."

"Mmm, hmm, night."

* * * *

Her gentle snores told him that she'd gone to sleep almost immediately. Not so him. He'd get up and take a cold shower in the connecting bath except he was afraid it might disturb her rest. Their weekend together had held everything he'd hoped for, and more. She was such a passionate lover, not afraid to give or to show him what *she* wanted.

Her gentle touch had become firm, heating his ardor and quickly arousing him beyond control. That had never happened to him before. Maybe it had something to do with the weeks of wanting and not having her. He'd been about to give up on ever being with her in an intimate sense when she'd suddenly done an about face. Man, oh man, was he ever glad she did. The memory of that first night would stay with him forever.

Giving up on sleep for the time being, he rose and dressed, then quietly slipped into the hall. He found Luke in the kitchen.

"Hey, I thought you'd gone to bed," Luke said.

"Yeah, I did, but I couldn't sleep. Everything quiet down here?" he asked, before Luke could come back at him with a smart comment.

"Yep, nothing to report. You really think Roy will try to finish what he started?"

"Better safe than sorry and, just for the record, yes, I think he'll try again. Keep your guard up."

"Will do. I did a walk through, locked up and secured everything for the night. I heard Charlie call in on your radio so I answered him. He said he'll be in shortly for guard duty tonight."

"Good. He's one of my best men. Cocky as all get out, but has a good ear and eye. He won't let anyone get past him."

"I told him I'd wait for him but if you're going to stay up…?"

"Go ahead. Go to bed. I'll wait for Charlie. I need to check in with the station anyway. Maybe they've already captured Roy or know where he is."

"Good idea. Good night then. Thanks, Blake. It's nice to know I can count on you."

"Always, Buddy," he said as he slapped him on the shoulder in farewell. "Always."

After Luke left, he called the station. Both fugitives were still at large. No one had seen any sign of Leroy or his cellmate, and the masked men hadn't left any evidence behind at the Sheriff's van or in the alley where they'd parked their vehicle. The investigation was at a dead end and would probably stay that way until they made their move. When that would be was anybody's guess.

Blake walked to the kitchen door and looked out, but couldn't see a thing, the night was so dark. He flipped the switch on the motion detector and the bright light startled Charlie as he came into view, about to knock.

"Hey, Boss. What cha looking for?"

"Just looking. Everything quiet out there?"

"Silent as a mummy's tomb."

Blake winced. "You've been watching horror shows again, haven't you?"

Charlie grinned. "Yep, love 'em. This one was extra gory with…."

"I get the picture. No need to go into detail. I get enough of that on the job, and so, might I add, do you."

"Ah, boss, it's just make believe. I can enjoy that part of it. What we have to do sometimes isn't so nice. No enjoyment in that, for sure."

"I know, and preventing gory things from happening is an important part of the job–like protecting Luke and his family."

"I'm on it, Boss. Slept all afternoon so I'm good to go. Where's the coffee?"

"I'll make a fresh pot and show you how in case you need more before morning. There are snacks in the pantry. Zakia said to tell you to help yourself."

He finished up in the kitchen, bid Charlie good night and, taking his two-way radio this time, climbed the stairs, hoping to get some sleep. When he opened the door, the hall light shone on his sleeping beauty. She'd kicked the blankets off and her top had ridden up, one rosy peak cheerfully exposed to his view.

He closed the door and walked to the bed, pulled the blankets up and tucked them in around her luscious curves. He kicked off his boots then lay down, fully dressed, on the cot, certain he wouldn't get any sleep tonight.

His thoughts centered on Sam and the terror she'd been through today. Damn! He forgotten to ask if Forensics had found anything on her truck or in the area of the crash that would help pinpoint the culprit. He was certain it had something to do with Roy, but without evidence, his conclusions and suppositions weren't worth a dime.

He tossed and turned for a while, eventually getting up to undress and crawl between the sheets. Their coolness combined with the fresh outdoorsy scent calmed him. The last thing he remembered was thinking of the woman with raven hair and amber eyes, peacefully asleep in the next bed.

COVERT MISSION: UNDERCOVER COP

Chapter Nine

Sam awoke from an exciting dream due to spasms of pain as she rolled onto her bad arm. She must have called out, because Blake was at her side in an instant. He flicked on the bedside lamp.

"What is it? Are you in pain?"

"Duh, Sherlock! Of course, I'm in pain. Excruciating pain. Where are my drugs?"

"In my pants pocket. I grabbed them when I went back downstairs, just in case. Hold on for a minute and I'll get one for you."

She heard the water running in the bathroom, and he came back with a glass of water and the promised tablet. "Thanks," she said.

He helped her to a sitting position, placed the pill on her tongue and held the glass to her lips as she drank, swallowing the medication. Then his strong arms eased her back down on the bed.

"Need anything else?"

"No, just some company until the meds kick in."

"No problem."

He perched on the edge of the bed, his hand resting on her thigh. Heat radiated out from that simple touch, engulfing her body in flames. Wow! Was that his effect on her or was she running a fever?

"Blake, were we good together? You know? On the weekend?"

He smiled and the twinkle she loved appeared in his eyes, turning them to a brilliant blue. "The very best! If it hadn't been for the hearing, I would've spent the day in bed with you."

"Is that all it is for us? Good sex?"

"That's a difficult question to answer, Sam. We've never spoken of love, if that's what you're asking."

Disappointed in his answer without knowing why, she delved deeper. "So it was just sex, wanting each other. Or just needing to get laid, period?"

She witnessed the fleeting expressions come and go on his face, anger, concern, desire. He still wanted her.

"Sam, it wasn't just sex. It was a meltdown. We were so hot for each other. The sex was the greatest I've ever experienced, and that has to mean there were feelings involved on both sides. Don't you think?"

"I don't know what to think. I only wish I could remember. My body trembles when you're near, heats up until I'm weak with yearning, with wanting. It seems to remember even though my mind draws a blank."

"Don't force it, honey. As much as I'd love to make love with you, I can be patient. Wait until you're feeling better and in less pain. We have all the time in the world and, when your memory returns, I'll still be here."

"Promise?"

He leaned forward and kissed her, a gentle, persuasive kiss that had her floating on clouds.

"That's a promise and I've sealed it with a kiss. Feel better now?"

"Yes, much. Can you hold me?"

"I am holding you."

"What I mean is, will you lie down here and hold me while I sleep?"

"For a little while," he said as he rounded the bed and climbed in beside her. He slid an arm under her and cuddled her close, her cast coming to rest on his chest.

"This feels nice," she said. Her eyes fluttered closed, and she slept.

* * * *

Blake awoke to a quiet tapping at the bedroom door. He carefully extricated his arm from beneath her sleeping form and slid from the bed, donning his jeans before opening the door.

"Sorry to wake you, but the station called. They said it was important," informed Luke as he passed him the portable phone.

"Thanks," he said. Then holding the phone to his ear, he spoke. "Northrup here. What's up?"

"Okay…yes…really?...that's great. Send the info to me via Luke's fax…555-4000…I'll read through the details and get back to you…good work."

He ducked back into the bedroom to finish dressing then went downstairs to find Luke. "We may have gotten our first break. Can I use your office? Dexter is sending a fax over as we speak."

"I'll come with you," Luke said, leaving his father and Charlie to guard his family.

Luke unlocked the door and bade him enter.

"You keep it locked?" he asked, surprised.

Luke laughed. "Yep, ever since I found the boys in here feeding toast into my printer."

"Oh, okay. Does it still work?" he asked, amused at the antics of the twins.

"Somewhat. I'll have to buy a new one soon though. Cleaned it out but I'm still getting the occasional grease spot on papers. There's your fax now." Luke crossed the room to fetch the papers.

Blake scanned each one in turn then passed them over to Luke. "The paint I scraped off the bumper of Sam's tracker came from a 2009 Hummer. The owner, a doctor in Calgary, reported it stolen early this morning. Police located it at a shopping centre near where they'd stolen it. The only fingerprints found belonged to Roy and his cellmate, but get this—the idiots who wore the masks discarded them along with the truck. Forensics is checking them for DNA as we speak." Blake smiled at his friend.

"That's good, but don't you have to match the DNA to something?"

"Yes, but it's evidence for when we do catch up with them. All part of the job of nailing their hides to the wall."

"So they're in Calgary?"

"Not necessarily. That's probably where they left their vehicle when they nabbed the Hummer. Left in a crowded parking lot, no one would notice how long it had been there. They could be anywhere."

Luke sighed heavily. "I'll be glad when this is over."

"Me too, buddy. We're working on it."

The fax machine rang again. Blake walked over to the machine and picked up the single sheet of paper. "That's weird. The hair fibers in one of the ski masks match those found embedded in the driver's seat."

"Maybe the owner of the Hummer is a ski fanatic. The Rockies have snow year round. There's quite a heli-business going on, or so I hear."

"Yes, I've heard of the elite few who fly to the top and ski down. Could be. Or it could be we need to run a check on this doctor. Find out what he's been up to."

"You're thinking he's involved? Why use his personal vehicle? That's a dead giveaway."

"Not if it's reported stolen before the crimes were committed. I'm going to call DuShane in Calgary. Run this info by him. If he thinks it's enough to go on, he'll run a check on the doctor and get a search warrant if necessary."

"Sounds like a plan. I'll leave you to it."

Blake thumbed his cell phone open and hit the speed dial number for DuShane's direct line. When he hung up a few minutes later, he faxed him the reports he'd received, smiled and left the room, locking it behind him.

He glanced at his watch and, realizing how long he'd been gone, took the stairs two at a time to check on Sam.

* * * *

It took Sam an awful long time to wiggle her body to the edge of the bed. She tried to put her feet flat on the floor and lever herself up, but when the door opened unexpectedly, it surprised her and she fell to the floor with a thud. "Ouch!"

Blake was at her side immediately. "Are you all right?"

"Sure! I love falling on my ass. Help me up, will you?"

He lifted her to a sitting position on the edge of the bed.

"I need the bathroom. Can you attach my arm so I can attend to…uh…things?"

He picked up the prosthesis and clipped it in place. "Need any help?"

"If I do, I'll holler." She walked to the bathroom and turned at the door. "You'll wait for me?"

"I'll wait right here," he said as he sat in the overstuffed chair by the window.

She opened the door a few minutes later. "Blake, do you think you could find me a plastic bag and some tape or something to cover my cast? I'd like to have a shower."

"I have just the ticket." He dug through his forensics kit, coming to her with a clear plastic bag in one hand and an elastic in the other. "How will you manage

119

with one hand?" he asked as he fastened the bag over the cast. "Now that it's cracked, wouldn't the water mess up the electronics?"

"Nope, it's a swimmer's prosthesis. And I've managed with one hand before. I just have to learn how to do it again." She smiled, proud to have this slice of independence.

"Well, don't lock the door, just in case," he said, concern etched into his handsome features.

"I won't. I'm not stupid. Besides, I might need you to wash my back." She smiled with impish delight when his mouth fell open, his eyes darkening with desire. It felt so good to be wanted, desired by this gorgeous man. Playfully, she blew him a kiss then went back into the bathroom, softly closing the door behind her.

She emerged a half hour later, quite pleased with herself. Not only had she showered and washed her hair, she'd dressed herself. Sort of. She'd pulled on her jeans, but couldn't do up the snap, and she'd pulled a shirt on over her cast, over her head, and got it stuck on her prosthesis. She hadn't bothered with a bra. She wasn't in the mood for self-torture today.

The look on Blake's face was priceless. His eyes fixated on her breasts, hanging loose below the top, he crossed the room, eased her backwards to sit at the edge of the bed and knelt in front of her.

His hands reached to cup their fullness, and he brought one to his mouth, laving and sucking on it until she was awash with sensation. He turned to the other breast, paying it the same attention. Liquid heat pooled at her core. She wrapped her hand around him to pull him closer, the broken, splinted finger tangling in his hair.

"Ow," he said.

"Sorry, I just…."

"It's all right." He reached behind his head to untangle her finger and held her hand once freed. "I'm sorry. I shouldn't have started this. You just looked so sexy, so delectable, I had to taste you."

"I'm not one whit sorry. I was trying to pull you closer when that stupid finger got all tangled up. Talk about a let down."

"Would you feel better if I finish what I started?"

"What?"

"Let me lock the door."

He did and came back to her, then eased her body down on the bed to remove her jeans. He kissed her then, a passion-filled kiss that left no doubt as to what he was feeling. His hands cupped and fondled her breasts, bringing her body to a fevered pitch of fiery need. When his hand moved to cup her mound, she arched her lower body to meet it. His finger entered her moist pussy, rotating and moving in and out, imitating the actual act. It wasn't enough.

"Fuck me, Blake. Take me now."

Instead, his head disappeared between her legs, and his tongue flicked out to lick her most private part. His hands moved beneath her ass to bring her closer to him, and he began to suck on her clit, all the while massaging her butt cheeks and getting closer and closer to the crack. When he touched her there, she exploded. Rocketing, rioting emotions surged through her as wave after roaring wave wracked her body.

Blake turned her so she was lying fully on the bed and went into the bathroom to return with a warm facecloth and towel. He wiped her clean and dried her, then pulled her jeans up over her legs as far as he could. Lifting her effortlessly, he stood her in front of him as he tugged her jeans up and fastened them. He slid her T-shirt over her head and straightened it into place.

"Where are your socks?"

"Where are my socks?" she asked. "Is that all you have to say?"

He kissed her, effectively cutting her off as her body swayed toward him.

"You're so beautiful and responsive to my touch, but I don't want you catching cold. So, where are your socks?" he repeated.

"Still in the duffle, I would imagine. I haven't unpacked."

He eased her to a sitting position on the bed and went to retrieve a pair of socks. He massaged warmth back into her cold feet before covering them in cloth. It felt divine! Shivers of awareness skittered along her spine, and she wanted nothing more than to lay with him, to make love with him.

"Blake?"

"Shhh!" His hands on her waist, he drew her forward and helped her to her feet. "We'll have time later to explore further, but right now, I need breakfast. You hungry?"

"Well, yeah," she said, curious as to why he didn't want her. He must need release, too.

"Then let's go downstairs. I smell pancakes."

"But you didn't…."

"I'm fine."

He hugged her one last time and kissed her forehead then steered her toward the door. She followed, still in an after-haze of fulfilled desire. What she wouldn't give to have more time with this wonderful man. More time and a lot less pain.

"Did you grab my pills?" she asked as they reached the landing.

"No, I forgot. Wait here."

He dashed back to the bedroom and reappeared in no time, bottle in hand. Together, they went downstairs and entered the kitchen. Blake's nose wasn't wrong. He found pancakes and sausage in a covered dish at the back of the wood stove. Of Luke and his family, they were nowhere in sight.

Blake seated her and then brought everything over to the table. He placed pancakes and sausage on her plate and cut it up for her. Then he poured their coffee.

She slathered butter onto her pancakes and smothered them with maple syrup. "Ummm, delicious!"

"Zakia makes the best pancakes I've ever eaten," Blake said between mouthfuls.

"I'd have to agree, even though I don't remember ever eating them before."

"Oh, you have." He chuckled. "She always makes plenty extra when you're around."

"Are you saying I'm a glutton?"

"Nope, just saying you love Zak's cooking."

"Oh! Okay. In that case, can I have another?"

He stood and prepared another plateful for her, snagging another pancake for himself before sitting back down. "Wait until you taste her potato pancakes. They are to die for."

"I'm partial to the blueberry myself." Her head jerked up to see Blake smiling at her. "I remembered!"

"Yeah, I caught that. Won't be long now and you'll remember everything."

"From your mouth to God's ears. I certainly hope He's listening."

Blake chuckled. "Time, Sam. Give it time. It's only been a day."

"Yeah, and I'm remembering bits and pieces here and there. I have to trust that the rest will come– eventually."

"It will, now eat up so we can go check on everybody. It's too quiet around here."

"Aye, aye, Sir. I'd salute but I'm holding my fork and wouldn't want it to go flying your way."

"You're excused this time, but don't let it happen again."

The mock silliness helped set the mood for a carefree day. Sam couldn't help wishing that they didn't have guard duty. All she wanted was to lead this man back to the bedroom and have her way with him. Tonight. She'd look forward to tonight. That might be the only way she'd get through today.

* * * *

Blake put away the breakfast things and stacked their dishes in the dishwasher before going outside. He led Sam over toward the barn, knowing her love of horses, and it was there they found Luke and the boys.

"Good morning, guys. Where's the rest of the family?"

"Mornin' Blake, Sam. Dad and Winnie went to town to get some grub. Don't worry, Charlie went with them," he added.

"And Zakia?"

"Zakia wasn't feeling too well this morning, so she went back to bed."

"Who's with her? I didn't see anyone else in the house."

"Well, you two were there, so I figured it was all right to lock up and bring the boys out to play with the puppies. They were getting kind of antsy," he said, a worried frown puckering his brow.

"I can understand that. Those two are so full of energy! It's hard to keep them cooped up. We'll head back up to the house. Next time leave me a note or something. Okay, buddy? She shouldn't be left alone.

After all, she was the main target," he said in a low voice so the kids wouldn't overhear.

Blake hadn't wanted to worry Luke, but leaving Zakia alone had caused a niggling sensation at the back of his mind. Something was wrong. He just knew it! "Come on, Sam. We need to hurry."

"Why? What is it?"

"Call it gut instinct, premonition or whatever. Zak may be in danger."

"Then go! Don't worry about me."

He ran to the house, palming his pistol as he entered through the kitchen door. The uneasiness was so sharp, he could feel it, almost taste it. He sniffed the air. Cologne, not his, and it hadn't been there when they'd eaten breakfast. Adrenalin told him to run to Zakia, but he didn't want to run into an ambush, so he checked each room as he went, cautiously approaching the stairs.

Up he went, his gun at the ready. His instincts proved correct once again when he found a man, dressed like one of Luke's wranglers, waiting in the master bedroom. The sounds of Zakia puking her guts out in the adjoining bath covered his near silent footfalls on the plush carpeting as he came to within a few feet of the stranger.

"Hands up!"

"What the fuck?" The man whirled toward him, gun in hand. One swift kick dislodged it and sent it careening across the room. He attacked, landing Blake a good one on the chin, but before he could get away, Blake delivered a quick left to his stomach then wrestled him to the floor. The man was strong, but Blake was in better condition, soon subduing the culprit face down on the floor with a knee to his back to keep him there.

"Blake, are you all right?" Sam asked as she suddenly appeared in the open doorway.

125

"Yeah, but get my cuffs will you? They're in my bag in the bedroom."

She returned in moments, and he handcuffed the man to a post on the bed.

"Go check on Zakia. She's in there being sick," he said as he pointed to the bathroom door.

She walked over and knocked, then tried the door. "It's locked," she said to Blake.

"That's probably what saved her hide just now."

"Stupid bitch picked a great time to get sick," said the prisoner, cursing a blue streak from his position on the floor.

"Shut up or I'll stuff your mouth with a dirty sock," Blake warned. "And this is Luke's room. After a day in the barn, they don't smell pretty."

The man spit at him in answer but at least he shut up.

"Zak? It's Sam. Are you all right?" she asked through the door.

The door opened, and a pale Zakia stood outlined in its frame.

"I think so. What are you doing in here? Who's that?"

'Haven't gotten to that yet. Do you recognize him?" asked Blake.

"I do," said Sam. "He's been to the shop before. One of my regulars. Tom something."

"I've never seen him before, but at least you've remembered something else," said Zakia, putting a comforting arm around her friend. "What's *he* doing in here?"

"He was waiting for you to finish being sick. Thank God you locked the door." Sam smiled, pleased with being able to remember her shop. Even the fact that she'd left Brogan in charge. "And yeah, remembering is great! Bits and pieces come to mind when I least expect them."

"Blake, do you think you could get that guy out of here? I need to lie down," asked Zakia as she leaned on the doorjamb.

"Of course. I'm sorry, Zakia. Just let me call in some back-up and I'll take him downstairs."

"Don't be sorry. I'm glad you got him and I hate to be a bother, but...."

"No bother." He used the two-way to call a couple of his men up to the house then left the room to lead his prisoner downstairs. "Sam, stay with Zakia until I get back."

She nodded and crossed to sit in the big chair beside the bed as Zakia lay down and pulled the covers over her shaking body.

"Are you cold? Do you need another blanket?"

"No, just reaction setting in. I'm shaking like a leaf in the autumn wind. To think that he got so close.... How *did* he get in here?"

"Miscommunication between Luke and Blake. I'm sorry, Zak."

"At least he arrived in time. I don't know what made me lock the bathroom door. I usually don't."

"Well, I'm certainly glad you did. Can I ask a question?"

"Sure."

"Are you pregnant?"

Zakia smiled beatifically. "Yes, and you are the first to know after Luke."

"Oh!"

"We didn't want to announce it to the world until all this was over, you know? Just one more reason for the family to worry and more leverage for the bad guys to use against us."

127

"This Leroy sure seems to have some seedy characters for friends," said Sam.

"The hardest part is not knowing who or how many."

"Yes, I suppose so. Look, do you need anything? Water, crackers, anything?"

"No, thanks. I have crackers in the nightstand drawer. I'll try those in a few."

"Okay."

Luke entered the room, his hands balled into fists at his sides and a worried expression on his face, the boys in tow and running straight for the bed. Sam took it as her cue to leave and slipped out into the hall. She managed to slide a chair from her bedroom into the hall, and there she sat until Blake returned for her. Zak was the best friend she'd ever had, well, as far as she knew. If all she could do for her was keep watch and holler an alarm, then that's what she'd do. That guy had gotten too close today…way too close. Thank the Good Lord for morning sickness!

Chapter Ten

Blake wanted to travel to the station with his prisoner and do the interrogation himself, but his sworn duty to protect the Mannings kept him at the ranch. He'd almost failed today. It wouldn't happen again! He had to keep his mind on the job.

Although, since being run off the road, Sam came under that umbrella, too. He needed to keep her safe, for his own benefit as much as hers. That man, Thomas Cremlin, as he now knew thanks to faxing a picture to Brogan, could have already been in the house during their early morning tryst. He'd concentrated so much on pleasuring Sam, nothing else mattered at the time. He shook his head to dispel her image from his mind; to dispel the look of rapturous amazement when she'd experienced that orgasm—her first since the bout of amnesia.

After seeing his prisoner off, he arranged to have two extra men in the house. There would be one on duty upstairs and two on guard downstairs at all times. He also assigned extra men to patrol the perimeter. He knew Roy and his men were in the area, and he wasn't taking any chances. Tonight he'd take a turn on duty at the back of the house, in the kitchen. Would Sam stay up with him or go to bed?

Damn! He couldn't keep that woman off his mind. It might be better to allow her time to get some extra sleep, thereby keeping his mind on the job. The problem with that was the fact that he'd still be thinking of cuddling up next to her. May as well keep her at his side. At least that way he'd know she was all right.

He went back inside to find Luke and the boys making sandwiches for lunch.

"Hi, guys. Need a hand?"

"Nope, almost done," said Luke.

Blake sniffed the air. "I smell peanut butter."

"And jam," said Casey.

"Umm, umm, my favorite. What's for dessert?"

"Chocolate chip cookies," said Cammy. "Mommy's sick."

"Yes, I know. Is she sleeping?"

"No, Sam's upstairs keeping her company. Dad and Winnie should be home soon. I'm going to volunteer her services for dinner if Zakia's not up to it," said Luke.

"Both are excellent cooks. Much better than eating my own cooking."

Luke gave him a strange look. "I've eaten your cooking many times. Nothing wrong with it."

"Yeah, I'm a fair cook, but Zakia has us all beat. If you don't need me here, I'll go check on the women."

"We just came down, and Pete's up there, but go ahead."

"I have someone coming to replace him and another to help out down here." He chose his words carefully due to the attention of the twins. He knew from past experience that those two listened to every word.

"Good, but no worries. I trust Pete."

"Okay, back in a few."

Pete sat in the upstairs hall, the ever-present knife and piece of wood in his hands. He leaned forward slightly so the shavings fell into a bucket on the floor.

"Hi, Pete! What cha working on today?"

"Bears."

"Bears? Why?"

"Well, I reckon the boys already have cows and horses. This time, I thought I'd make them some bears."

"I know they carry those horses everywhere. Didn't know about the cows. You're quite the craftsman."

"Nah, just something to do when I'm waiting around."

"Well then, have fun."

He crossed the hall and knocked on the door to the master bedroom.

He heard Zakia bade him, "Come in." So he opened the door and walked in. Sam was talking to someone on the phone, and he went to sit beside Zakia. "How are you holding up?"

"Better now, but Luke blames himself for that guy getting in here. Can you set him straight?"

"Can do. Don't worry about it." He nodded his head in Sam's direction. "Who's she talking to?"

"Brogan called here when he couldn't reach her on her cell."

"It's probably still in the truck. I'll check on that for her."

Sam hung up and turned to them with a wide smile on her face. "I guess I still know how to run the business," she stated proudly. Then she glanced at Blake, concern and confusion evident in her expressive, amber eyes. "So why can't I remember you or the accident or my past? This doesn't make sense."

"Time, Sam. When the time is right, your memory will return," he said, trying to reassure her the best he could. "Luke and the boys have prepared us a feast for lunch. Any takers or do I get to eat your share?"

"I'm coming," said Zakia, smiling as she sat up to put on her slippers. "I wouldn't miss their peanut butter and jam sandwiches for anything."

Sam and Blake both chuckled.

"I didn't say what they'd made."

"You didn't have to. With those two boys of mine, it's either pizza or peanut butter and jam whenever they get to choose. I know we don't have any frozen pizza, and Luke's never made one, so…."

"Brilliant deduction! Shall we go?" asked Blake.

"Bring me back one of those sandwiches, will ya?" Pete asked as they headed for the stairs.

"You bet!" said Blake.

In the end, the twins took lunch up to Pete. Having already wolfed down their own sandwiches, they were ready to run and see what he was whittling for them.

* * * *

Lucas and his wife arrived home while they we're drinking their after dinner coffee.

"It took you long enough. I was beginning to worry," said Luke as he stood up from the table.

"We stopped at our spread on the way into town. Had to pick up a few things we forgot," said his father.

"Next time call or I'm going to get you a cell phone so I can track you down."

"I don't want one of those gall-darned things. Besides, Charlie had one. If you were that worried, why didn't you call him?"

"Harumph! Never thought of it or I would have."

Blake joined the Manning men as they left the kitchen. They brought in groceries and had them put away in no time at all. His cell phone rang so he excused himself and stepped outside just as Luke began relating the day's events to the elder Mannings.

"Northrup here."

He listened as his deputy relayed the news. Cremlin wasn't talking.

"Did you run his prints…any matches? Really? That's interesting. Well, at least we know he was at the scene. We can charge him for two counts of attempted murder and two first degree for the shooting of the

Sheriff and his deputy. Maybe that will get him talking…okay…yes…good job."

He went back inside to find all eyes on him as his friends waited on his news. "Well, the prints we picked up off the undercarriage of Sam's truck match the guy who was here today. His blood matched a sample found in one of the masks and, get this, he lives in the same neighborhood as the man with the Hummer. Now, I don't hold much interest in coincidence, as you all know. It's clear we have one of our suspects from both crime scenes, but we don't know if he's our main man or a hireling."

"What do we do now?" asked Sam.

"We do what we have been doing–stay on guard. If you see, hear, or smell anything out of the ordinary, I want to know about it. Any other questions?" All five heads shook in the negative. "All right, then. I need to call DuShane in Calgary and see what he found out today. Luke, can I use your office for that? It's a lot quieter in there."

"Sure thing," Luke said as he dug the key out of his pocket.

He entered the office and made the call only to find that the doctor checked out squeaky clean and the judge wouldn't issue a warrant. Darn!

Next he called the impound yard and informed them that the Hummer was important evidence in an ongoing investigation and asked them not to release it. They already had. The owner had picked it up about an hour before. Damn! What was going on?

First, his evidence wasn't good enough to get a search warrant, now it was disappearing. His only hope was that Forensics had done a thorough job on the Hummer. He called the lab.

Fibers found in the back seat matched prison issue clothing, added proof that Roy and his cellmate were in that vehicle. It hadn't been hotwired. No forced entry.

What the hell? Who leaves their keys in a vehicle as expensive as a Hummer? An unlocked one at that! This entire thing just does not compute.

The lab technician was still talking. "I'm sorry. What was that you said?"

"Embedded in the tires was a mix of animal feed, corn, a clay type mud, and elk feces."

"Elk? Are you certain it isn't something else?...Okay...Yeah. Keep me posted when you find out. Good job!"

Blake hung up the phone deep in thought. The Hummer belonged to a city man, a doctor. The escape happened on a city street and the vehicle later abandoned in the city. Where would it have picked up those samples? He called DuShane again to discuss the latest info.

The Hummer was reported stolen at seven thirty-five a.m. yesterday morning.

The Sheriff's van was hit at eight twenty.

Evidence, namely the masks, placed the Hummer as the getaway vehicle.

Evidence, the blue paint, placed the Hummer as the vehicle that ran Sam off the road. Given the time of her phone call to Zakia, she should have arrived at the ranch around eleven thirty. He'd found her around three that afternoon.

The Hummer was found abandoned at a Calgary shopping centre early that morning.

The samples they'd discovered in the tires would suggest an agricultural area.

"DuShane, they could've been anywhere, but I'm thinking that Williams knows all the back roads leading to the Thunder Creek Ranch, since he used to work here."

"Yes…I'm not sure. I've never heard of elk roaming this area, but it's possible. Yes, I'll check with the Mannings and get back to you on that. Yes, we have a surplus of guards in place. Thanks, I appreciate the offer. Yes, they could be holed up on the ranch. It's a big spread with some heavily wooded areas…roger that. I'll alert my men. We'll be careful."

Blake cradled the phone and went looking for Luke and his father. Luke was still in the kitchen, but his father and the women had left.

"Where are the others?"

"They went to the living room to watch TV."

"Good! Luke, how many line camps are on this property?"

"One each in the east, west and northern sectors. Why?"

"Would Williams know a back way to reach one of them?"

"It's pretty rough country out there, but there are well-worn trails. Yeah, he'd know."

"Would those trails be wide enough for a Hummer?"

Luke slowly nodded his head. "Yeah, there's a cut-off on Highway One, west of Calgary, which we sometimes use in the winter. We keep it wide enough for the tractor, so a Hummer would fit. Do you really think he'd be brazen enough to camp out on my property?"

"It's looking that way. Next question, do you take feed out to those northern pastures?"

"If any of the herd is out there, we do. That area is mostly clay and grass doesn't grow too well."

"Have you ever seen elk in the area?"

135

"Yeah, I've seen the odd one or two at the river. Why the inquisition?"

"The Hummer's tires had feed, clay mud, elk feces and…." He consulted his notes. "Corn embedded in the treads. Had me wondering where it had picked up that combination."

"I think you're on to something, Blake. The feed we use is mixed with corn, kind of a silage blend for more nutrition. I'd say Roy's there, at the line camp, biding his time. Probably caught one of the horses and using it to get around. No motor to cut the silence."

"Hadn't thought of that but you're probably right. What I can't figure out is his connection to Cremlin, the man we caught today."

"Who knows? Roy always did hang out with some pretty shady characters. So, what's the plan?"

"Highway One comes under Calgary's jurisdiction. I'll call DuShane and see what he advises. If he takes that on then we don't have to leave the ranch house virtually unguarded."

"Good thinking, but you know my men are eager to help."

"Yes, but I prefer to have the law tackle this. Don't want any civilians getting hurt on my watch." He grinned at Luke then went back to the office, his call to DuShane acquiring the desired result. When he turned, Sam, looking hot and sexy, stood in the open doorway.

"What's the smile for? Did they catch him?" she asked, moving close enough that he could smell a faint whiff of her perfume.

"Not yet, but DuShane's arranging a S.W.A.T. team to raid one of Luke's line camps."

"What's a line camp? And why would they want to raid one of Luke's?"

"Line camps are strategically placed around a property this size so the wranglers can hole up there in case of emergency. We think Williams might be staying in the northern one. I have to get directions to all three from Luke, just in case."

"He just went in to watch TV with the others. Want me to send him in?"

"That would be great! Thanks."

She leaned forward and planted a swift kiss on his lips, surprising him.

He caught her around the waist as she started to turn away. "What was that for?"

"Nothing in particular. I just felt like it," she said, telltale color filling her cheeks.

"Good, because I've wanted to do this since you appeared in the doorway." He hauled her close, careful not to hurt her arm, and kissed her. All the pent up need, longing and frustration at their situation transferred into a blazing hot, mind-numbing kiss of pure pleasure.

When he came up for air, he was glad to have the support of Luke's heavy mahogany desk behind him. Weak at the knees and dizzy with desire, he longed to take her right there and then. He held her close, her head resting against his heart, the beats pounding through his brain like a wild drum solo.

"As much as I enjoy holding you, I have work to do."

"I know," she said, pulling away. "I just needed a quiet moment with you. I'll send Luke in. See you later."

"Later, yes. I'll see you later." Geesh! He sounded like a parrot, or a bumbling idiot. He wasn't sure which.

Luke came in and drew out a rough map of the property showing the position of each camp. Blake faxed it to DuShane then called to make sure he'd received it.

He also found out that S.W.A.T. was set to go in at midnight, hoping to take them by surprise.

"Are you sure they won't get lost out there?" Luke asked.

"Nope, but they do have night vision goggles, so I'm hoping they'll find their way in and out okay."

"Why not let me go out and lead them in?"

"Not a chance. You're one of the targets, remember?"

"Yeah, but I hate sitting and waiting for something to happen. I'd rather be doing something…anything."

"I hear ya, buddy, and you are doing something. You're helping to protect your family. I need you here."

Zakia stuck her head in the door. "Luke, I wanted to let you know that Winnie and I are going to the kitchen to start dinner. The boys are playing in their room but would you mind going up to check on them? It's not like them to remain quiet this long."

"I'll head right up. Need anything else before I go, Blake?"

"Nope, but I'll be in the kitchen keeping an eye on the women if you need me."

He entered the kitchen and double-checked the window and door locks before grabbing a coffee and taking a seat at the table. "Where are Lucas and Sam?"

"In the living room playing a game of chess."

"Chess?"

Zakia smiled his way. "Yep. She recognized the chessboard and wanted to find out if she knew how to play. Lucas took her up on it."

"He would, the old scoundrel. Wants to play a little kick-ass game, does he?"

"Oh, I'm sure he'll take it easy on her," said Winnie.

"He doesn't know how. That's why he earned the title of District Champion."

"Well, it will certainly test her skill at the game," said Zakia.

"That it will. I think I'll trade places with Scott for a while. At least I can watch their game from the front entry. Might prove entertaining."

Zakia chuckled softly as she peeled potatoes. "Yep, it just might."

Scott eagerly switched places. "Thanks, Boss. I'm dying for a cup of coffee."

"No problem. Fill your boots," he said as he shooed him on his way.

Blake checked the window for any movement outside then settled in to watch Sam, deep in concentration as she studied the board, as was Lucas. Finally, she moved her knight into position.

"Harumph! Didn't expect that one, Lassie," Lucas said. "Now I have to sacrifice either my Rook or the Bishop." He studied the board.

Blake saw his hand reach toward the Bishop, moving it out of harm's way. Sam played her Knight and took his Rook. Play continued as each studied the board, cautiously planning their moves until, at last, Sam said, "Checkmate." She'd won.

Her exultant smile was something to see, lighting up her features with a radiant glow that highlighted her high cheekbones. Her amber colored eyes appeared orange, their similarity that of glowing embers. Beautiful! Good for her! She certainly hadn't had much to smile about lately.

COVERT MISSION: UNDERCOVER COP

Chapter Eleven

"Rematch, best out of three," said Lucas.

"Oh no you don't," said Winnie, as she approached from the direction of the kitchen. "Dinner is ready, and I refuse to make everyone wait because of your compulsion with winning. Good job, Sam! He doesn't get beat often enough and I'm afraid it goes to his head." She smiled, taking the sting out of her words.

"Maybe after dinner?" Sam ventured.

Desire swamped Blake as he continued to watch Sam sparkle, making it almost impossible to speak. He cleared his throat. "Sam, I'm doing the night watch tonight, so I'll have to get some shut eye after dinner. Did you want to stay on shift with me or keep regular hours?"

"Oh, I'll stick with you. Sorry, Lucas. Some other time?"

"Sure, Lass. Sure."

They entered the kitchen, and Scott immediately rose to his feet and assumed a position at the front of the house. Winnie took a dinner tray up to Pete and called Luke and the boys to dinner. It was a boisterous meal, and Lucas took some good-natured ribbing for losing at chess.

By mutual agreement and out of concern for Winnie, Blake and Luke said nothing pertaining to the proposed raid later that night. Luke volunteered to remain at the rear of the house with one of Blake's men, pulling guard duty until Blake came back down. He wanted to be on hand when the men reported in.

Replete with all the excellent food Winnie and Zakia had cooked up, he skipped his after dinner coffee, content to go upstairs, knowing he'd sleep. Then again, with Sam so close, sleep might not be an option. He smiled to himself as he followed her upstairs. That curvy tush of hers was pleading to be touched.

Nope! He needed to sleep if he was supposed to stay awake from midnight until dawn. They entered the bedroom and he allowed her first use of the facilities. Big mistake! She came out wearing the sexiest lingerie he'd ever seen.

Dark purple, almost black, except when the light hit it; then it shimmered and shone like the purest satin. The bodice and sleeves were lacey—almost see through, the straps securing the top tied at the nape of her neck. How did she manage that with one hand?

The bikini panty was high on her thighs, showing a gorgeous expanse of firm, tanned skin. Strings dangled from her hips and his fingers itched to pull at them, to untie those cute, silky bows and watch the skimpy fabric drop to the floor.

He finally looked up—into the face of the woman whose body displayed such nightwear to perfection. Desire flared in the depths of her eyes…desire for him. She didn't know him, couldn't remember him from Adam, and yet she was willing to give herself to him. Why? Payment for services rendered that morning? No, he didn't think so.

"Sam, darling, you are gorgeous!" He opened his arms and she flew into his embrace, burrowed her head into his chest.

"I thought…. I didn't know…."

"What did you think?"

"I was afraid you'd think it silly of me to want to wear this for you, you know…with the cast and all. Yet when I found it in my duffle this afternoon, I had to. It looks new. I think maybe I bought it to wear for you."

"Ah, Sam, I'm honored. You look very sexy in that outfit, so much so that I didn't even register the cast or prosthesis. You are one hot bundle!"

"Really?"

"Yes, really." He kissed her then, all restraint disappearing in the haze of passion that ensued. One hand snaked between them to fondle her breast through the silky lace, the nipple peaking as he rolled it between his thumb and forefinger. His hand moved down to cup her mound, rubbing the heel of his palm against her, delighted when he found it already dampening with need.

He pushed the flimsy lace aside so he could feel her, and pressed a finger inside to stroke her warm, wet passage. She gasped and her insides tightened around his digit. He continued his stroking until she relaxed against him, then added another, working them in and out in a rhythm as old as time; a rhythm matched by their tongues as they mated and withdrew, mated and withdrew. When she reached her climax, the juices gushed out in a steady stream as she vibrated against him. Only when the trembling ceased, did he remove his fingers, pick her up, and carry her to the bed.

"Good night, my sweet. Sleep well," he said as he carefully tucked her in.

"Blake? What? Why...?" Her face wore a look of confusion, a frown furrowing her brow.

"Not tonight, Sam, as difficult as it is to not climb in beside you. We have to be awake and alert in a few hours. No hurried couplings for us. I won't compromise on our lovemaking or our safety."

"Can you at least hold me?"

"Not if I'm to preserve my sanity." He laughed, gave her a quick kiss on the tip of her nose, then undressed and crawled between the sheets of the cot. His cock rock-hard and aching, he thought sleep would be a long time coming, but tonight, the habits of the job kicked in. Whenever he was on assignment, he slept wherever, whenever. He slept and dreamed of a luscious, dark-haired beauty wearing nothing but purple lace and a contented smile as she rode his white stallion into the sunset.

* * * *

"I dreamt I was screwed," she said later that evening as she sat with Blake while he was on guard duty.

His head jerked sideways, and his mouth dropped open as he stared for a moment at the woman who constantly invaded his thoughts. "Geez, woman! You sure don't hesitate to say it like it is. By who?"

"You."

"Uh…was this a good screwed or a bad one?" he wondered uneasily.

"Oh, it was good. Very, very good," she said, her eyes focused on his crotch.

"Sam, does this mean you've remembered us…together?"

"No, it means I dreamed of us together, and I woke up hornier than hell. What are you going to do about it?"

Her challenge was one he desperately wanted to take her up on, but they were on guard duty. It would prove a distraction that could cost them their lives. "There's nothing I *can* do about it. At least, not right now and not until you're well. I don't want you coming out of this bout of amnesia thinking I took advantage of you."

"Not even a quickie on the kitchen table?"

He glanced at the ranch's kitchen table, solidly built of heavy oak. Her thought did have merit, but what if someone came in? "We're not the only ones in the house, you know."

"Yeah, I know. Makes for more excitement, don't you think?"

"Aw, Sam, you're killing me here. We can't do this. Maybe when we go off duty."

"Maybe I won't be horny then," she pouted.

He reached out a hand to smooth her long hair back over her shoulder, cupped the back of her neck, and drew her forward for a swift kiss. "When we make love again, I want the warm, willing woman I had before. I want you remembering how good we are together. Understand?"

"I'm *hot* and willing. Isn't that better?"

He smiled. "That's good but not necessarily better. Our time will come. After all, you remembered Zakia and the twins, chess and blueberry pancakes. Give it time."

She rose to cross the room when a gunshot sounded. The kitchen window burst inward, shards of glass flying everywhere.

"Sam!"

She'd fallen to the floor but raised her head up slightly. "I'm not hit, but help me up will you?"

Without the use of her arms, getting up from a prone position would be nearly impossible. Crouching next to her, he helped her to a sitting position, her back against the cupboard. A hurried banging at the door caught his attention. "Blake, it's me, Charlie. Everything okay in there?"

He went to the door, careful to stay out of sight of the windows, unlocked it and ushered him in. "We're fine. Thanks for getting here so quickly. Did you see who it was? Where did the shot come from?"

"We didn't see anyone but the shot came from the far side of the barn. Half a dozen men are in pursuit, but it's a dark night. I don't hold out much hope of them catching whoever it was."

"Maybe they'll get lucky."

Their attention diverted by a ruckus in the yard, Charlie reached for the doorknob.

"I'll go check it out, boss."

"Be careful out there."

"Always am. Be right back." He grinned and was gone.

Charlie was one of those guys who lived to see action, thrived on it, but he wasn't careless. For that, Blake was extremely thankful.

True to his word, he returned a scant ten minutes later. He was grinning from ear to ear.

"Well, that's one scoundrel we don't have to worry about anymore. Made the mistake of crossing the pasture where Luke keeps his bull. Gored him up pretty bad."

"Did he give his name?"

"Nope. We called an ambulance. Scott and Louis are going to ride in with him. Keep him under guard."

"Good work, Charlie. They probably won't try anything else tonight, but wake a couple of Luke's men to replace Scott and Louie. We can't let our guard down now."

"Okay, boss."

"See if you can find something to cover the window. Plastic and a couple of boards will do for tonight."

"Saw a roll in the barn. I'll fetch it for ya."

Blake helped Sam to her feet then went to the pantry where Luke kept a household tool kit. He loaded a staple gun with staples, grabbed a hammer and a fistful of nails and popped back into the kitchen in time to admit Charlie again. They made short work of covering the window and, after Charlie left, Blake locked the door and cleaned up the broken glass. It wouldn't do for one of the twins to hurt himself on a stray sliver.

"I guess you were right," Sam said from her position at the table.

"Right about what?"

"You know, about us, about getting screwed. We need to stay alert."

He kneeled beside her and locked his eyes with hers. "It's not because I don't want you. I do."

"I know," she said with a cheeky grin. "But my timing sure leaves a lot to be desired."

"That it does. How's the arm?"

"Still attached." She laughed as the words left her mouth, and he smiled.

"I wasn't asking about the prosthesis. Did you jar the cast? Are you in pain?"

"No more than usual. I'll survive."

Suddenly, a sad look crossed her features.

"What is it, Sam? Did you remember something?"

"Not really, but I feel like I've said those words before. It's as if they hold some kind of meaning for me."

"Perhaps they do," he said, unwillingly to bring more pain to light. "If so, you'll figure it out when your memory returns."

"Yeah, I guess so."

The bright flare from the hall light warned them of someone approaching. Blake rose to face the door, relieved to see Luke enter.

"Man, you must sleep awful sound. You missed all the excitement."

"What excitement?" he asked, looking around. "What happened to the window?"

"A bullet came zinging through a couple of hours ago, but we got the culprit. Or, I should say, Old Red got him."

"Old Red? What? How?"

Blake filled him in while Luke put on a pot of coffee.

"Well, sounds like you two have had quite a night. Seeing as I'm up, you may as well crash for a few."

"Don't you have chores to do?"

"Not today. Cal's in charge. I decided to take the day off and spend it with the family."

"Want me to call one of my men in for back-up."

"No need. Dad will be up soon. We'll manage."

"DuShane hasn't reported in. I'd like to stay up and find out what went down, but I'm bushed. I'll say good night then, or good morning." He laughed and turned toward Sam, already on her feet and looking exhausted. "Come on, beautiful. Time to get us some shut eye."

With the rifle in one hand and his free arm around his woman, they left the room and made their way upstairs. He glanced at the cot, placed in her room so he could attend to her needs. It didn't hold much appeal.

"Blake, will you hold me tonight? I don't think I'll sleep otherwise."

He groaned inwardly. How could he sleep with her and not touch her? Not make love to her? Already his cock was perking to attention. "Do you think that's wise? What if I roll over and hurt your arm?"

"You won't. Is that the best excuse you can come up with?"

"No excuses, just stating the facts."

"Then come to bed."

Heaven and hell. It was heaven to hold her next to his heart but hell on his libido. Oh well, he'd survived worse and, closing his eyes, he slept.

* * * *

Sam awoke from the most delicious dream in which Blake played a huge part...very huge. His erection was poking her from behind, probably the reason for such a vivid dream. She giggled softly, not wanting to wake him, but try as she might, she couldn't slide out from under his arm. Part of her rejoiced that he'd hold her so tightly, even in sleep, but she needed the bathroom in the worst way.

"Blake?"

"Hmmm."

"I need to get up."

"Hmmm."

"Blake, I have to get up, now," she said with a little more emphasis.

"Why?"

"Bathroom."

"Oh!" He rolled over onto his back and rubbed the sleep from his eyes. The sheet slipped down to his waist and she drooled, wanting to see more. Needing to know if her dream was just that or a memory. Morning stubble added a rakish look that, combined with his unkempt hair, had her wanting to mount up and ride. He flipped back the covers and rose from the bed–to her disappointment, in boxer briefs. Darn!

"Blake, are you well-endowed?"

He swiveled toward her. "What?" he asked in astonishment.

"Down there," she nodded at his crotch. "Your manhood, cock, dick–whatever you want to call it. Are you?"

"What brought this on?"

"It's only a question. Can't you give me a straight answer?"

"Why do you want to know?"

"I dreamed of us…uh…together, only I think it may have been more of a memory."

"Is that so? Where did this dream take place?"

"I don't know. We were in a bed but the rest was in shadow. So *are* you?"

He grinned. "Of course I am!"

"Really?" she asked, her interest perking up.

"Woman, there isn't a man alive who would answer that question in the negative."

"Why not?"

"Ego, pride–take your pick."

"Okay then, let me ask this a different way. Are you hung like a horse or a puppy?"

His rich laughter rang out, filling the room. "I'm hung like a horse. Wanna see?"

"Oh, yeah," she drawled.

A commotion outside drew his attention. All of a sudden he was all seriousness as he crossed to look out the window.

"What is it?" she asked as she rolled to her side and levered herself up on her stumpy arm, using it to support her as she shifted her body to the edge of the bed and stood.

"DuShane's here along with half the Calgary detachment. This doesn't look good. If you can manage all right by yourself, I'll see you downstairs."

"I'm fine. Go."

He pulled on his jeans and boots, grabbed a shirt and his gun and left the room. She stood by the bed, staring at the closed door when it suddenly reopened. Blake crossed the room in two strides, lifted her cast and took hold of her hand, slid her fingertips down his hard length. He leaned forward then and kissed her, hard and swift, before letting go.

"Does that answer your question?"

Before she could articulate an answer, he was gone.

Wow! He really was hung like a bloody horse!

Grinning like a love-struck teenybopper, she headed for the bathroom, the scorching dream still fresh in her mind. *Maybe dreams did come true!*

* * * *

Blake met Luke in the hall.

"I was just coming to get you. DuShane's here."

"So I noticed. Has he said anything?"

"Didn't ask, although Dad probably has by now. He went out to meet him, but I thought it best to alert you first."

"Thanks, buddy. Let's go."

Sure enough, Luke's father was grilling DuShane when they joined up with him in the yard. And since neither he nor Luke had confided in him concerning the raid on the line camps, he was justifiably angry.

"Sorry, Dad, but it could've been a wild goose chase. No sense getting you and Winnie worked up," Luke said.

"I suppose, but a man has a right to know what's happenin' on his own land."

"Yes, you do, Mr. Manning, and I apologize as well," said Blake. He turned to the new arrivals. "What's up, DuShane? I take it they weren't holed up at any of the line camps."

"No, they weren't, but they had been. Plenty of tracks in and out of all three. I'd say someone tipped them off."

"As you just heard, Luke, myself, and Sam were the only ones aware of your plans. If there's a leak, it had to come from your end."

"Damn! I was afraid of that. Internal Affairs has been doing some investigating, but it's all been very secretive. Not so much questioning anybody in particular as just hanging around, listening in on everyone's conversations."

"We'll worry about that later. You said there were tracks at all three? Any clear enough to cast?" Blake asked, earning a smile of admiration from the city cop.

"Yes, we also found prison issued clothing and fingerprints all over the place. Dirty cups and glasses." He smiled. "If any of them have a record, and we know two do for sure, we'll have plenty of evidence to place them at the scene."

"Did you get my report on the man we captured yesterday?" asked Blake.

"Yes, Thomas Cremlin. He's from Calgary. I've dealt with him before. He has a rap sheet a mile long, but until now it's only been petty theft and vandalism. This changes things. I'd like your okay to question him before returning to Calgary."

"No problem. I'll call it in. We had another incident last night. The man is in hospital in Fort Macleod."

"What type of incident? What happened?"

"A man took a potshot through the kitchen window and ran off."

"How did he end up in hospital? You caught him?"

"No, actually, Luke's bull did. Let's just say he picked the wrong pasture to run through."

DuShane laughed, his hearty laughter breaking the tense formalness of their meeting.

"So what now? Why the troops?" asked Lucas Senior.

"We need to continue the search. I don't think they've gone far. I rallied my men as quietly as I could so as not to raise any questions. Luke, is there any place else on your property where these men could hide out?" DuShane asked.

"Geez, DuShane! There are thousands of acres out there." He thought for a moment. "There's a ravine, quite deep, due west of the homestead. A river runs through it but it's dried up until the fall rains start. It would offer good cover and protection from the wind. The foothills of the Rockies begin on the other side. They could find any number of places to hole up, but it's getting mighty cold at night. They'd need heat, a campfire."

"How accessible is this ravine?"

"Roy knows the way in. We had some cattle trapped down there when he worked the ranch. I can lead you there."

"I prefer not to have civilians along. It would be better for you to give us the co-ordinates and a map of the land if you have one."

"No problem, I can get that for you."

"Anything else I should know about the area?"

"Yeah, if it starts rainin', get the hell out. I'm not likin' the looks of those clouds, and that river is known for flash floodin'," said Lucas Senior.

"Okay, thanks. Consider us warned. Blake, where are your men stationed?"

"In the house, bunkhouse and barn, out of sight."

"It might be better for now to have them clearly visible, or at least, most of them. If we flush these guys out, they could head this way. A show of force might deter them."

Blake nodded. "Point taken. I'll rally the troops and post them around the perimeter of the house and yard until you report back."

Two tractor-trailers pulled into the driveway, diverting their attention. Blake cast a questioning look at DuShane.

"Our horses have arrived."

His men moved as one to intercept the trucks. They had the horses unloaded and saddled up in no time at all.

"I'll get that map," said Luke and headed for the house.

"As soon as you're mounted up and on your way, I'll organize my men, but I'll be keeping two in the house and a couple of sharpshooters in the barn."

"Good call," said DuShane.

"Good luck," said Blake. "I hope you find the bastards."

Luke returned with the promised map and went over the lay of the land. DuShane nodded and mounted up, his men following two-by-two.

"Now what," asked Luke.

"Now we put our men into position and we wait," said Blake. He walked to the barn to gather his men while Luke headed for the bunkhouse.

Chapter Twelve

Blake instructed his men to ride the perimeter, approximately five hundred feet away from the ranch house and buildings. If Roy or any of his cohorts made a move, they were to fire three shots in warning before closing in. Charlie and Jake would be in the house and his sharpshooters, Neal and Fred, were in position inside the barn. Luke's men would patrol the house and grounds–a second barrier, just in case.

With everything as ready as it could be, Blake and Luke went back inside the house. Sam was at the table, nursing a cup of coffee, the evidence of a late breakfast in front of her.

"Hi, Luke, Blake. Zak's in the living room with the boys."

"Thanks," he said as he headed in that direction.

"Hello, gorgeous! Save any food for me?" he asked.

"No, but Zak left some on a plate in the oven for you. I think she was afraid I'd eat it all."

He opened the oven door to find a plate piled high with French toast, sausage lining the side. "If you're still hungry, I'll share."

"No, I'm good."

She smiled at him over the rim of her cup. Her eyes seemed more whiskey-colored at that moment, rich and full of mischief.

"What have you been up to?" he asked as he slathered his French toast with homemade strawberry jam.

"Nothing much. Did you know Zak's writing a cookbook?"

"No." A short answer between bites, but damned if Zakia didn't make the best French toast he'd ever eaten.

"Well, she is, and the recipes seem awful easy. I thought maybe I'd try one, you know, as a side dish for dinner."

He almost choked on his food, sputtering and gasping for breath, trying not to laugh. "Uh, did you mention that to Zakia?" he asked, knowing that Sam wasn't much of a cook.

"No. Why?"

"Well, she might take offense to someone else in her kitchen," he said, for lack of any kind way to deter her.

"She lets Winnie. Why not me?"

"True, but you're still recovering. Wouldn't it be kind of difficult for you?"

She turned her head sideways to gaze up at him. "Blake, you're fudging. What are you *not* telling me?"

He sighed and plunked down his fork. "You can't cook."

"Why not?"

"I mean, you really *can't* cook. You stink at it. You always laughed and said something about 'burnt offerings' whenever you'd tried."

"Oh!" Her face fell. "I just want to be useful, you know?"

He stood and rounded the table, hauled her to her feet and held her close. "Sam, you're not useless. You've suffered a setback, but you're the most independent woman I know. I'm happy you've allowed me to help you through this and I'm sure Zakia feels the same."

"Really? I'm not a burden?" She pulled back far enough that she could look him in the eye.

"Not at all," he answered sincerely. "Just having you near helps me get through the day. I wish circumstances were different, but we'll cope."

"I saw DuShane and his men ride out; the extra patrols you put in place. What's happening?"

"He found evidence that Roy and his crew had been using the camps, but they'd scattered before his team arrived. DuShane thinks, as I do, that they may still be holed up nearby. They're riding out to search the ravine and, if nothing there, the foothills."

"How long will that take?"

"Depends on their success. It might be all over today, or it could be a few more. I'm hoping for today."

"Yeah, me too. Zakia's kind of nervy. She tries to hide it, but I know her so well. I feel for her, especially in her condition."

"What? What condition?"

"Oops! Sorry! Not my story to tell."

"Is she pregnant again?" he asked in a hushed whisper, his mouth close to her ear.

"Yes," she whispered back, a happy grin flitting across her face. "But I didn't tell you," she warned.

"No, you didn't. I'd already guessed something was afoot, what with her sick every morning." His own grin widened at the image of how Sam would look, growing large with his child. He loved children and intended to have plenty. Growing up alone certainly wasn't any fun. His mind wandered to Luke's twins, Casey and Cammy. Those two always had each other to play with. And the mischief they got into…well, he had to chuckle at them. They never meant any harm, just two little boys out to garner their share of attention.

"What's with the silly grin?"

He thought fast. "Just imagining Luke being a Daddy again, this time with dirty diapers and all."

She giggled and cuddled back into his arms. "Zak sure had her hands full with those two. That I can tell you."

Blake's beeper went off, the sound strange to his ears after not hearing it for days. "I need to call the station," he said as he thumbed his cell open and walked out on the back deck. "Northrup here. What's up?"

"Yes…really…well, I'll be damned....Yep, thanks for filling me in."

The screen door creaked behind him. He whirled to see Luke standing a few feet away.

"Sam said you might have some news, so she came and got me."

Blake grinned. "Smart girl. I've had some news, all right. It seems Old Red took out Simon Clarke, Roy's cellmate. A real badass as per reports and the charges he's up against. I'm glad he's out of the way, but I do have to wonder how many men were involved in the escape."

"I've been wondering the same thing. There had to be at least three–the driver, the two shooters, and possibly a look-out."

"Any more than that and they would've been tripping over themselves to get in the Hummer and get away from the scene," mused Blake.

"Yeah, so with Cremlin and Clarke out of the way, we have Roy and maybe three others. Good odds."

"Unless they're part of a gang that we don't know about. So far, my men haven't found anything to link Roy with Cremlin and Clarke, but it's there. Has to be."

"What about the doctor who owns the Hummer? Where does he figure in all this?" asked Luke.

"DuShane couldn't find anything on him, and the judge wouldn't approve a search warrant on our suppositions, no matter how convincing they were. He appears to have an excellent reputation and an airtight alibi during the escape, so that clue ended up a dead end."

"Harrumph! Alibis can be bought. What was his?"

"He was performing surgery at the time."

"Damn it, Blake! I want an end to this. My family has been victimized long enough."

"I hear you, Luke. We're doing everything we possibly can. We'll get him."

"I know, Blake. It's just that I worry about Zakia, the toll this is taking on her. Hell! We've another child on the way and can't even rejoice in the fact."

"Congratulations, old buddy," he said, slapping Luke on the back in a friendly gesture. "Looks like you've still got it in ya."

"Yeah, but we've been keeping the news to ourselves. If we announced it to all and sundry, it would only give Roy and the like more leverage. Might even drive him over the edge if he still thinks Zakia should be his."

"Yes, that is a worry. Does your father know?"

"Nope."

"Because of Winnie? Roy being her son?"

"Yep! That's it in a nutshell. I hate this!"

"It's a tricky situation, for sure. Let's hope DuShane and his men get lucky."

Luke ran troubled fingers through his already wind-tossed hair and stood looking out over the field. "What if they don't?"

"Then we continue as is. We'll get him, Luke. Bank on it."

"Yeah, I've got to get back to Zakia and the boys. Keep me posted."

"Will do."

Blake watched him reenter the house, wishing there was more he could do. He was glad they were safe, but something would happen, and soon. He could feel it in his bones.

* * * *

Luke rushed through the kitchen as if the hounds of hell were at his heels. Sam poured another coffee and pushed her way out the screen door.

"Here. I thought you could use this."

"Thanks," said Blake, taking the proffered mug. "Bad news?"

"No, good news, just not good enough."

"Oh."

"Luke's of the same frame of mind as I am. Won't be happy until these guys are all behind bars."

"I can understand that, especially after hearing that bullet come zinging through the kitchen."

His beeper sounded again....

"It's the station. Excuse me a sec." He dialed the phone.

"Northrup here...who...what did he want...what did you tell him...? Good. Thanks for the heads up."

"Hmmm, that's weird."

"What is?"

"Some guy called my detachment, claiming to be a judge. He's looking for DuShane."

"Did he say why?"

"No, but I'm wondering if I should ride out and notify DuShane. It could be important."

"If it is, he would've left a message. How would he even know DuShane and his men are down this way?"

Blake gave her a fond look bordering on admiration. "Good question, Sherlock. How would he know? DuShane hinted that no one knew of their whereabouts, so what gives?"

He seemed lost in thought for a minute or two, so Sam stood quietly, waiting.

"I wonder if it's the judge that refused the search warrant on the owner of that Hummer? He knew we were working together on this case. Maybe he had a change of heart."

"Or maybe he just likes keeping tabs."

"Damn! I wish he wasn't so far away. If I'd known sooner...."

"You would've had your answers. Patience. He'll be back."

Blake finished his coffee and set the mug down on the rail, then pulled her into his arms. "You're right. All we can do is be patient and wait. Like you said, if it was important, he would've tried to get a message to him."

"Did your man tell him he was here?"

Blake chuckled. "Couldn't, he didn't know."

"That might be for the best."

"How do you figure that?"

"Well, he wouldn't be the first corrupt official to gain office of some kind. As a judge, he wields a lot of authority."

Blake held her at arm's length, a stunned expression on his face. "Damn it, girl! That's it! I need to make a phone call."

While he spoke into the phone, the wind picked up speed, the heavens opened and rain, badly needed, poured down in driving sheets. They scurried into the house where they could watch the deluge happening and remain dry. His call completed, another theory being investigated, Blake seemed to relax somewhat.

Things were starting to come together in his investigation by the sounds of it. For that, she was extremely thankful. She hated seeing him so tense.

If only her memory would return. Maybe then, she could be of some help to him. Why, oh why couldn't she remember?

* * * *

The afternoon was quiet, although entertaining, as Sam proudly whomped Lucas's butt at chess. They'd played three games, and she'd bested him two out of three.

"Where did you learn to play so good?" asked Lucas.

"In the army," she replied without thinking.

"Lots of time on your hands? Oops, sorry, lass! No offense."

"None taken. We didn't have much spare time, but the doctor I worked with was a competitive player. He taught me to play so he could keep his skills in practice."

"He taught you well."

"Thank…ow!" She pressed her fingertips to her temples.

"Sam! What is it?" Blake heard her talking about the doctor and knew it was only a matter of time until she remembered the sad outcome of their affair. "Are you all right?"

"Blake, my head hurts…real bad. Could you help me upstairs so I can lie down?"

"Sure, sweetheart. Lucas, you okay to stand guard for a few?"

"No problem. Take care of your woman."

He picked Sam up and carried her upstairs, kicked the door fully open so he wouldn't bump her cast, and laid her gently on the bed. "Do you want one of your pain pills?"

"No, but a cold facecloth might help."

"Coming right up."

When he returned, she was sitting on the side of the bed, tears streaming down her face.

"I remember, Blake." She sobbed uncontrollably for several minutes.

He sat at her side and wrapped one strong arm around her. "What do you remember?"

She grabbed the facecloth and swiped at her eyes. "Everything...Dr. Paul, as we called him, my baby–everything."

"Oh, honey! That's the one memory I wish I could've spared you."

He hugged her tight, his arms a comfort she couldn't afford, not now—now that she knew. She pulled away to search his face, saw the caring concern registered there and knew she had to put a stop to it...to them.

"No, I needed to remember. I don't want to hurt like that ever again."

"If it's within my power, you won't ever hurt that way again."

"Thank you for that, but I'm a good example of fate playing a hand...or losing one." She hiccupped a laugh. "I won't risk it again."

"What are you saying?"

"You and me. There's no us. No future for us together. Better that you know now."

"I can't accept that, Sam. We have something really good going between us. We need time to see where it goes...see what develops."

"Nothing will develop. We are not going anywhere. The sex has been great, but that's where it ends. Has to."

"Give me a chance to change your mind. When this is over...."

"When this is over, I'll be going home–to Calgary." She stood and crossed to the bathroom, but

163

before she closed the door behind her, she said, "Don't fight me on this, Blake. I don't have the energy."

The door closed then and the lock clicked into place. She'd shut him out. He didn't understand it. After all they'd been to each other, after all they'd been together, she was walking away. Women! Would he ever understand one of the creatures?

He stood, about to leave the room, until he realized that she might have also recalled the accident that sent her speeding into the ditch. He sat and waited.

She emerged, eyes red-rimmed from crying, from mourning her lost lover and child no doubt, while here he sat, mourning a love that never had a chance of surviving.

"We need to talk," he said.

She nodded and sat in the chair by the bed.

"Do you remember the accident that made you leave the road?"

"Yes. As you said, it was a big, dark blue Hummer. It followed me down from Calgary, but I hadn't paid much attention, until it turned off the main road and continued to follow me down the five-nineteen. The next I knew it rammed me from behind, and I fishtailed a short distance. Then, I sped up, knowing that if I made it to the ranch, I'd be safe.

That's when he pulled up alongside me and I glanced sideways, straight into the barrel of a forty-five. I stomped the accelerator and yanked hard to the right, misjudged my distance and left the road. One of them came to check on me, but I pretended to be dead– unmoving, scarcely breathing. Very difficult to do when what you really want is to crawl out and away from a crashed vehicle. I was afraid it might explode. The smell of gas was so strong."

"What happened then?"

"He pounded on the window, but I never moved, so he must have been satisfied that I posed no threat. He left. Once I heard the truck take off, I leaned forward to turn off the key. The movement caused the pain in my head and arm to explode, and I must have passed out. The next I knew, I was waking up at the side of the road on a stretcher."

"Okay, let's backtrack a bit. You said you faced the barrel of a gun. Did you see the man holding it? What did he look like?"

"Yes, I caught a brief glimpse." She closed her eyes and leaned back in the chair. "Blond, wavy hair, about shoulder-length, clean cut, blue, blue eyes. The top of his head disappeared above the window frame, so he must be quite tall. Wore a white T-shirt." She opened her eyes. "That's all I remember."

"That's excellent. Do you think you'd recognize him if you saw him again?"

"Yes. I don't think I'll forget him...ever." Then she laughed. "Well, I guess I did for a while there."

He chuckled, glad to see her sense of humor surfacing. "Is there anything else you remember? What about the driver? Could you see him at all? Were there others in the vehicle?"

She sat straight up. "The driver! All I saw was his hand on the steering wheel, but he had a huge, silver ring with a black stone on his right hand, ring finger. He also sported a really gross snake tattoo. It was black and yellow, fashioned as if wrapped around his arm with the fangs pointed toward me."

"Anything else?"

"No, and I didn't see or sense anyone else in the vehicle."

"Could you draw that snake for me?"

"Uh, no-o," she said, holding up her arm. "This thing isn't much good for holding a pencil."

"Sorry, I forgot. What about Luke's computer? Have you ever used a drawing program?"

"Yes, I've fiddled around with it some. I could try."

"Good! Whenever you're ready, come downstairs. I'll get the key and wait for you in Luke's office."

He stood and left the room, hoping her drawing skills were adequate enough to have the design traced back to its artist.

Luke was in the barn doing chores while the boys played with Luke's round-up dog, Rounder, and her puppies. Good, he'd be able to speak with Luke without them overhearing…he hoped.

"Hi, guys! Those pups sure are getting big."

"Yep!"

"And they like us, too."

"They sure do. Have fun." He walked past them to where their father worked further down the aisle. "Mucking out stables. I'd offer to lend a hand, but I need your office key."

Luke pulled off a glove and reached in his pocket then passed Blake the ring of keys. "What's up?"

"Sam's memory came back. She's going to try to draw what she saw with the help of your computer."

"She must be relieved. Sure, go ahead."

"Thanks, buddy."

When he arrived at the office door, Sam was already there and smiling.

"Did Luke ever tell you why he keeps the door locked?" she asked.

He grinned in response. "Yes, those boys can be little mischiefs at times."

Sam laughed as she entered ahead of him and crossed to sit behind the desk. She powered up the computer and searched through the programs until she found the one she wanted. Opening a blank page, she began to draw, haltingly at first, then with sure, fairly smooth strokes.

"Hey, you're really good with that mouse," he said from his position behind her.

"Thanks," she said without looking up. "I started playing around with drawing on a computer to help improve the flexibility in my hand. It takes a lot of concentration to move the muscles that control the prosthetic."

"I'm impressed!"

"You're also distracting."

"Want me to leave you alone?"

"No, just quit hovering."

He laughed and rounded the desk to sit in the chair facing her. Big mistake. He seemed to be full of them lately. With nothing to occupy his time, he drank in his fill of her.

Her long, dark hair hung loose these days, probably too difficult for her to tie it back one-handed. It was in sharp contrast to her fair complexion. She resembled a porcelain doll: perfect to look at, but cool and hard to the touch. At least, that's how she'd seemed earlier.

Not so last weekend. Then she'd been alive with a passion that matched his own, soft and yielding, yet aggressive and adventurous by turns. What happened to make her back off? Was it their disagreement at the courthouse?

He opened his mouth to ask her then promptly shut it again. Engrossed in her drawing, he didn't want to disturb her. This would be important evidence, if she could get it right.

Chapter Thirteen

It would be a hell of a lot easier to concentrate on what she was doing if Blake wasn't in the same room, but she enjoyed his company, even when he quietly waited for her to produce results. The drawing was taking shape, the snake almost three-dimensional, its demeanor fierce and foreboding. Now she had to color it in.

"I just remembered, the pretty man, the one with the gun? His skin was tanned, dark, as if he'd recently returned from a vacation somewhere."

"Could he be naturally dark-skinned?"

"Could be, but somehow I don't think so with that light blond hair."

"Can you draw portraits, by any chance?"

She paused to glance up at him, smiling as his question produced instant images in her mind's eye. "Yes, actually, I'm a damned good portrait artist."

"Fantastic!" His eyes blazed a brilliant sapphire as his excitement rose. "I'm going to owe you big time for this."

She turned back to her work. "You've taken care of me since I got hurt. You don't owe me anything. Besides, I want to see an end to this stalker business, too."

He rose to stand in front of the window. She couldn't help but watch. Every move he made was so graceful, like a dancer, yet he was all honed muscle, ready to pounce, to protect those in need at a moment's notice. He stood tall, his back straight, his Levi's snug, outlining his ass cheeks to perfection. She found it hard to believe that she'd never touch those drool-worthy buns again, never mind what nestled on the other side.

Fate was a bitch! Why couldn't she give her a break, allow her to be heart whole and fancy-free? Sam asked herself how could she allow one freak accident to change the course of her entire life? Did she really want to grow old alone? To never experience passion again? Or the satisfaction that comes from giving as well as receiving pleasure?

With Blake, she'd have everything her heart desired, or almost. But she'd be short-changing him on the life he had mapped out for himself. No, if she couldn't have Blake, she wouldn't settle for second best. He was a decent, caring man, deserving of everything he wanted in this life…something she couldn't give him. Something she'd known from the moment she saw his house. She dropped her head and tried to focus through the tears welling up in her eyes. *Concentrate, damn it!*

Her hand trembled on the mouse as she pushed it around, the picture coming to life before her glazed eyes. She paused for a moment and rubbed them dry, then looked again. She'd done it.

"Blake, I have it. Come see."

She tilted the monitor up for him to get a better look.

"Geez! If the gun hadn't scared you, that snake sure enough would. You're amazing!" He kissed the top of her head and gave her a quick hug. "Want to take a break or start on the man?"

"I'm good. The sooner I finish these, the sooner you can send them off."

"I intend to run them by DuShane first. He might recognize the tattoo or the man."

"Okay. Whatever. Now go sit. Or better yet, fetch me a coffee. I'm running low on caffeine."

"Your wish is my command. Be right back."

* * * *

Zakia was in the midst of dinner preparations, and the coffee pot was empty. "Mind if I make a pot of coffee? I don't want to be in the way."

"Nonsense," she said, smiling at him. "Help yourself. There are cookies in the pantry if you need something to hold you over until dinner's ready. I wanted to call you two for lunch, but Luke said you were working on something important."

"Luke was right, but thanks for thinking of us." He grinned as he filled the pot with water. "Where is Luke? He should be here with you." Blake frowned, realizing she'd been unguarded.

"Nature call. He'll be right back."

"I'll wait with you until then. Until this is over, you shouldn't be alone at any time, especially downstairs."

"Yeah, I know, but…."

"No buts. He should have called me or one of the men, seeing as how you've been the main target all along."

"I'm so tired of all this. When will it end, Blake? When?"

"Soon, Zak. Sam's memory returning gave us a big advantage. She saw one of the men and a tattoo on the other. She's in there drawing them now."

"She's quite an artist. I don't know how she does it."

"Neither do I but I'm glad she's so good at it."

Luke came back and Blake busied himself pouring coffee. On his way out of the kitchen, he said, "Next time you want to pull a disappearing act, call me."

"Sorry, but…."

"Uh, uh. No buts. Her life is on the line. Remember that."

Suitably chastised, Luke took it in stride. "Point taken."

Blake nodded and returned to the office, and Sam. She barely glanced at the coffee, just picked up the mug, took a sip, and put it back down to continue working. He glanced at the screen. The man looked familiar. Why? Where had he seen him before?

"I know that man," he said.

"You do?"

"Well, I know I've seen him before. I'm trying to place him."

"Wait until I've finished these final details. Maybe then you'll know. In the meantime, go sit."

"Okay," he said, the image playing on his mind as he drank his coffee. "Damn! I forgot the cookies."

"What cookies?"

"Zakia thought you might be hungry. We missed lunch."

"We did?" she asked, her head turning toward the wall clock. "Yeah, I guess we did. I'm not that hungry. I'll wait until dinner."

"So will I, then."

He sat in silence, waiting and thinking. He never forgot a face. That's one of the things that made him so good at his job.

"Finished!"

"Already? What have you got?" He rose to stand behind her and couldn't believe his eyes. "That's Kincaid, Roy's lawyer."

"Well, well, well. Ain't that interesting? Small world, isn't it."

"It sure is, sweetheart. It sure enough is. I can't wait to show these to DuShane. Come on. Let's grab another coffee and sit outside for a spell."

"Sounds good. Let me save these first." She pressed a couple keys, shut down the computer, and rose to her feet. Picking up her mug, she smiled, pleased with what she'd accomplished. "Lead the way!"

* * * *

Daylight ended early at this time of year. Blake escorted Sam out onto the back patio where they sat comfortably in a two-seater swing. He pushed off gently, careful not to slop their coffees, and they sat in companionable silence watching the sun disappear behind the horizon. The rain they'd had earlier had already soaked into the dry earth without a sign of the drenching they'd received, almost as if it had never been. Tonight's sunset was a brilliant display of reds and yellows, harbinger of a beautiful day on the morrow. The night was mild for autumn, the air brisk and refreshing.

His thoughts returned to his earlier conversation with Sam. Somehow, he had to find out what prompted her to break off their relationship before it had really begun. He understood her not wanting to be hurt, but without risk, there was little reward. Surely, she realized that he'd never cause her any harm.

"It's beautiful out here, quiet and peaceful, far different from life in the city," she said.

"I wouldn't trade it for love nor money. My spread may not be as big as this one, but it's beginning to show a profit. A few more years and I'll be able to retire in style."

"Really? Somehow, I can't see you pushing your cop persona to the background. It's so much a part of who you are. You're a protector, someone who actually *wants* to right the wrongs of this world."

"Thanks, but as a cop, I see too much, have lived through too much. Some days, it just gets to *be* too much. You know?"

"Yes, I do. I've seen my share of fighting and war, senseless acts of violence against the innocent. Nothing much surprises me anymore."

The rocking motion of the swing calmed his mind as well as his body. He sipped his coffee, wondering how best to approach the subject of them together. Spending his life without her wasn't an option. She meant too much to him. Should he just come right out with it? Tell her how he felt? This compulsion to spend twenty-four/seven with her ate at his heart and soul. Was it love? It certainly felt like it.

Suddenly, three shots rang out in rapid succession. "Hot damn! They've sighted them."

"Who? DuShane and his men? Was that the signal–those shots?"

"Not necessarily DuShane, but yes, those three shots were a signal that someone has spotted the outlaws. My men in the field will be in pursuit, and Luke's men will close a tighter circle around the house and grounds so nobody can get through."

"Good, I'd hate to see Zakia or the twins get hurt, or anyone else for that matter."

She rested her hand on his knee, the cast felt heavy, but it warmed him that she'd make a move, any move, to touch him.

"I'm glad you're here and not out there somewhere."

"Why?" he asked, hoping...needing her to confirm her feelings.

"Why? What a weird question. With you sitting right here, I don't need to worry about my friend being shot or killed?"

"Would you worry? Would you miss me? Do you really believe we can go on from here as friends?" He removed her hand and placed it in her lap then stood. "I won't pretend to know what's going on in your mind, Sam. I don't have the foggiest, but I won't–can't–settle for friendship when I need so much more."

He descended the steps into the yard, his lengthy strides carrying him far and fast. The lump in his chest hurt as fierce as any physical pain ever did. She would be the death of him yet. He needed to walk, to think. He always did his best thinking while out and about on the range. A single shot rang out into the silence of the surrounding night. His chest hurt even worse. It took him a few moments to realize he'd been hit. Damn! He fell to his knees and collapsed face first in the prairie grass.

* * * *

Sam sat watching his departing figure disappear into the darkness, wishing with her entire being that she could be his. To spend the rest of her days in the safety of his arms would be heaven for her, but selfish, knowing what she knew. If she told him, he might still try to change her mind, only to regret years down the road when their love wasn't enough anymore. No, best to leave it as is. She'd survive; he'd find someone new and live a happy life. That's what she wished for him, but her heart hurt at the thought, as if it was breaking in two.

She struggled to her feet and pulled the screen door open. She had just stepped into the kitchen when she heard the shot–a shot that was too close for comfort.

"Luke!" she screamed.

He came running. So did the rest of the family and the two guards. "What is it? What's happened?"

"I heard a shot, and Blake…Blake's out there somewhere. We have to do something."

"Was Blake hit?"

"I don't know."

"Stay here. Lock the doors and don't let anyone in. Dad, you okay helping with guard duty if I take Charlie with me?"

He patted the gun in a holster on his hip. "Been ready. Take care out there."

"I will. Lock up and take everyone upstairs. Come on, Charlie."

"I'm coming with you," said Sam.

"No way. Blake would have my hide."

"He may be hurt and I have first aid training. You may need me."

Luke nodded. "Come on then."

The three of them stepped out the door, Sam bringing up the rear.

"Which way did Blake go?" Luke asked.

"Down the main trail past the barn," she answered.

The men eased forward, pistols in hand, staying in the shadow of the buildings as much as possible. Sam's heart thudded heavily in her chest as she followed. Some inner demon tormented her with a vision of Blake, lying cold and lifeless on the ground. He'd been the target of that single shot. She knew it. Felt it. And it was all her fault. If he hadn't been so annoyed with her, he wouldn't have gone off like he did. And, if he *was* all right, he would've come running back to the house when that shot rang out. She knew it and so did the others.

A rustling up ahead warned them of others approaching before they actually saw them. Then they heard a horse's clip-clopping hooves on the gravel. Someone must have sensed their presence for a small flashlight switched on. Its beam was aimed directly at them.

"Luke?" asked one of the men.

"Yeah, that you Cal?"

"Yep, your Buddy's hurt. We draped him over my horse."

"Take him to the house. Sam, go with him. Call an ambulance. Anybody see or go after the shooter?"

"One of Blake's sharpshooters had those fancy night vision goggles on. He saw the whole thing and went outta here lickety split," said Cal. "Hasn't returned yet, though."

"Well, we can't track him in the dark," said Charlie. "Team up and close in around the house. Stay alert. Make sure no one gets through."

Sam heard the men talking as she walked away, their voices carrying clearly on the night air, but her concentration was focused on the horse and its precious burden. She kept stumbling in the dark, falling behind and then rushing to catch up. It seemed to take forever to get to the house. She groped her way up the steps and banged on the door. Lucas and the other guard, Seth, let her in then went outside to help fetch Blake.

They carried him in and laid him on the sofa while she dialed the emergency number. She told the dispatcher what had happened and requested an ambulance, giving the address and particulars. The dispatcher continued to ask questions.

"Look, lady, I have a man bleeding to death here. Send help." She hung up the phone and raced to Blake's side. She was only doing her job and Sam felt bad for cutting her off, but Blake was her priority. He needed her.

Checking his pulse, she was relieved to find it slow but steady. She sent Lucas for a pan of warm water and some clean cloths, ripped his shirt open, and cleaned the wound as best she could, then held a steady pressure on it to staunch the bleeding. Thank God he was out cold, otherwise he'd be in so much pain she wouldn't be able to control the flow of blood. He'd lost so much already.

177

Sirens blared in the distance, and she breathed a heart-felt sigh of relief. Lucas opened the front door and let the paramedics in then walked up behind her and hauled her to her feet.

"Come on, Lassie. We need to stay out of their way so they can do their job."

"I know, Lucas, but I don't want to leave him."

"We're not leavin', just steppin' back a pace or two to give them room."

She allowed him to lead her to a chair by the fireplace, but its meager warmth didn't reach her. Lucas piled on a couple more sticks and had it blazing in no time. It didn't help. Cold seeped into her bones, dreadful cold, a cold like she'd only felt once before.

Please, God, don't let him die. I can't lose him, too.

She begged and pleaded, prayed for God to spare Blake's life, barely aware of Lucas draping an afghan around her shoulders. The paramedics checked his vitals and loaded him onto a stretcher. When they headed for the door, she rose to her feet.

"Sam, where are you going?" Lucas asked.

"With Blake." Two simple words that held a wealth of meaning. "I'm staying with Blake." Forever, if–no, *when* he makes it through.

The hospital staff was ready for him. They rushed him through emergency, gave Sam an envelope containing his personal belongings, and wheeled him into surgery. She was left cooling her heels in the waiting room. She drank cup after cup of bitter coffee as she sat and sobbed her heart out or paced the floor waiting for news.

A ringing sound came from the envelope. She picked it up and took out Blake's cell phone. "Hello," she said in a strained voice shaky with nervous worry.

"Yes, this is Blake Northrup's phone…no, he's not available at the moment…. Sam Muldoon, who are you…? Officer DuShane, he's in surgery…. He was shot." Her voice broke and she paused a moment, taking deep breaths to calm herself and listened as he filled her in. "That's good. Too bad it hadn't happened a couple hours sooner… Yes, I'm sorry, too…. No, there's nothing you can do, thanks…. Will you be going to the ranch…? Yes, Luke and his family need to know that it's over…. Thank you for letting us know. I'll inform Blake as soon as he's awake…. Good night."

It seemed a hollow victory, especially with Blake lying on an operating table with doctors fighting to keep him alive. She was happy for an end to it for Zak and her family, but at what cost? Pocketing the phone, she crossed to the window and stared out into the dimly lit parking lot. He'd been in there for hours! How much longer? It didn't matter. She wasn't leaving here until she could see Blake, talk to him and know he's all right.

Please let him be all right!

She didn't know how long she stood there until the door opened, and she turned to see Luke and Zakia. Tears started anew as they rushed toward her and enveloped her in a comforting embrace as she sobbed uncontrollably. Her sobs gradually lessened, and they led her to a chair, taking a seat on each side of her.

"You haven't heard anything yet?" asked Zakia.

"Not a word since they wheeled him into surgery."

"But that was hours ago!" said Zakia.

"I know," she said, gratefully accepting the tissues Luke handed her.

"I'll go see if I can find out anything," said Luke.

"Won't do you any good. Every time I've asked, they've given me a cup of coffee and told me to be patient a little longer. At least, knowing he's still in there, knowing the doctors are still working on him, at least I know he's still alive. Part of me is dreading the arrival of news."

"I'll try anyway. I could use a cup of coffee."

She hiccupped a laugh. "I gotta warn you, it's worse than Cook's bitterest brew during the round-up."

"That bad, eh?"

She nodded.

"Here, I've brought you something to eat," said Zakia.

"I'm not hungry."

"Maybe not, but you need to keep up your strength. Blake doesn't need to be worrying about you when he wakes up."

Sam was glad to hear the "when" not "if" and opened the dish to find cold slices of roast beef nestled amongst a creamy potato salad. "Maybe I will try a few bites." She picked up a slice of beef.

"Oh, I forgot." Zakia rummaged in her purse and brought out a Ziploc bag with fork and knife inside.

"Thanks."

Luke disappeared and came back a while later with three steaming cups of tea.

"Heaven! Where did you have to go to find this?" Sam asked.

"I asked at the nurses' station, and they steered me to the mini kitchen around the corner."

She took a sip, allowing the hot, milky liquid to soothe her dry throat. "Thanks, Luke."

"No problem."

"Did they offer any info about Blake?"

"Not a word."

"Figures."

When the door opened again, a man in green hospital scrubs and cap stood in the opening. He wasn't smiling.

"I'm Dr. Forsythe. You're here for Blake Northrup?"

"Yes. How is he?" asked Luke.

"He made it through surgery, but the bullet severed an artery and punctured his lung. The next twenty-four hours are critical. He'll be taken to Intensive Care once he's out of recovery."

"Thank you, Lord!" said Sam as she rose to her feet. "Can I see him?"

"In a few minutes. We need to get him settled in the Intensive Care Unit. I'll send the nurse out for you. One at a time. Be warned though. He's hooked up to life support systems and monitors. It looks more scary than it actually is at this point."

"Thank you, doctor," said Luke.

"My pleasure," he said and disappeared.

Sam sat down and broke into tears again, renewing tears, happy tears, thankful tears.

"Are you all right, Sam?" asked Zakia.

"I…I'm…f..f..fine," she said, smiling and crying at the same time. "J…j…just fine."

The nurse showed up about a half hour later. "Is there a Sam here?"

"Yes, that's me," she said as she stood on shaky legs.

"Mr. Northrup is awake, and he's asking for you. Come this way, please."

"Thank you."

All three followed the nurse down a labyrinth of hallways and through a set of heavy, double doors and finally reached his room in the ICU. He was laying there looking so pale and hooked up to so many bags and machines that it resembled something straight out of a horror movie. Her hand flew to her mouth, and she hit herself in the chin, forgetting all about the cast on her arm. She felt Luke's arm come around her, additional strength and support she needed badly. Then she straightened her back and grappled with her self-control before approaching the bed. It wouldn't do for him to see her so distraught.

"We'll wait in the hall," Zakia whispered.

Sam nodded.

Blake must have sensed her presence, because he turned his head toward her, opened his eyes, and smiled a wobbly smile. "I knew you'd come."

His voice muffled due to the oxygen mask, his breathing shallow and raspy, she had to stand close to hear his slow, stilted words.

"Come? I've been here all along. How dare you go and get yourself shot. I was so worried." Her voice wracked with emotion, a testament to how worried she'd been, she swiped at a stray tear and reached out to rest her hand in his.

He smiled that sad, wobbly smile again. "I love you, Sam." He paused. "I almost didn't get a chance…to say the words, so…I'm saying them now."

It was a real effort for him to speak, which made the words more intense, more endearing.

"You big oaf! Don't you think I know that already?"

"Just…makin' sure."

"And I need to do the same. I love you, Blake. I tried not to, but I do."

"Is loving me…so bad?"

"No, but the thought of losing you was hell." She smiled at him and eased onto the side of the bed.

"You haven't lost me…. I'll be up and…bugging you to make…an honest man of me…before you know it."

Tears welled up in her eyes. "Is that a proposal or the drugs talking?"

"I reckon…that's a proposal…. Marry me, Sam?"

"Yes, oh yes!" She leaned forward and kissed him soundly, relishing the life-giving force that allowed him to kiss her back.

"I have to go now, you need rest, but I'll be back."

"Okay. Promise?"

"That's a definite promise."

She walked backward until she got to the door, unwilling to take her eyes off the man she loved. His eyelids fell and she knew he needed rest. Finally, she turned and walked out. The nurse directed her to the ICU waiting area, and she felt as if she was walking on clouds all the way there. She took a seat as if in a daze and said nothing.

"Well, how is he?" asked Luke.

"We're getting married!" was all she could think to say.

Zakia squealed and wrapped her arms around her. "Congratulations!"

"I guess this means he's okay," said Luke, wearing a sarcastic, lop-sided grin.

"He's alive. That's okay in my book any day." Sam couldn't stop smiling even as tears of happiness streamed down her cheeks.

"Zakia, did you want to see him next?" asked Luke.

"No. You go. Say hi for me. I'll stay with Sam."

When Luke returned, the three of them left the hospital, headed for Thunder Creek and some much-needed sleep.

Chapter Fourteen

Dr. Forsythe arrived in Blake's room shortly after Sam arrived the following day.

"Good morning, Blake, and you as well, Miss. I must apologize. We didn't get around to exchanging names last night."

"No apology needed. I'm Samantha Muldoon, but my friends call me Sam," she said, extending her hand.

"Blake, I've come to explain how I went about fixing you up. Is it all right if she stays?" he asked, nodding his head in Sam's direction.

"Yes, Sam is my fiancée. She needs to hear this, too."

"Congratulations, then! Well, the short of it is this; the bullet missed your heart by the merest fraction and punctured a lung instead. I was able to perform a thoracotomy, fancy word for cutting out that part of the lung, and insert a chest tube to keep the lung inflated and allow for drainage. You'll have difficulty breathing until such time as I can remove it. It will be painful, but I encourage you to breathe deep and often to prevent fluid build-up in the lung. Any questions so far?"

"Yeah, when can I...go home?"

The doctor laughed. "Glad to see you have a good sense of humor after undergoing major surgery. I suppose you've been aware of the nurses coming in to check your bandages and monitor the drainage. That's what this machine is for."

He indicated a machine on the floor next to the bed that had tubes attached to it. She could easily see the bloody drainage and measurement indicators.

"Depending on how soon you heal, you could be here three days to a week, maybe more. Are you a smoker?"

Blake shook his head.

"Good! Someone will be in soon to take some chest x-rays to make certain the lung is staying inflated. Nurse will bring you a breathing machine and show you how to use it. You will need to take ten deep breaths every hour while you're awake."

"So how long do the tubes stay in?" asked Sam.

"As long as the lungs are draining, they stay. They can usually be removed the second or third day after surgery."

"When can I get up?" asked Blake.

"Nurse should have you up walking around by this evening. Any other questions?"

Sam looked at Blake to see him watching her. He shook his head slowly. "No, no more questions."

"Great! I'll see you tomorrow."

Blake rested after the doctor left, and Sam dug out the paperback novel she'd borrowed from Zakia, settling back in the armchair to read. A couple of chapters in, she was thoroughly hooked. She was also dying for a cup of coffee. She knew better than to ask the nurses, not after the wicked brew she'd received the night before. Blake still slept soundly, so she went to the cafeteria, deciding to grab a bite to eat as well. Before going back to Blake, she refilled her coffee and purchased a package of cookies to munch on later.

The "x-ray in use" sign hung on the door so she waited outside until the technician wheeled his cart out into the hall.

"Hey, handsome! How ya feelin'?" she asked in a phony western twang.

"Better, but can you raise the head of my bed so I can see you?"

"How about if I move the chair around to the side? We'll ask the nurse if it's all right the next time she comes in."

"Okay. What are you reading?'

"A romantic suspense. Why?"

He started to laugh which was the wrong thing to do. He coughed and sputtered and choked and she scurried to the bed to push the button for the nurse just as one rushed in.

"Now, Mr. Northrup, you need to lie still," she admonished as the coughing subsided. "Here, take a sip of water. Your throat is probably dry from the oxygen."

Sam knew full well that the problem wasn't a dry throat. His eyes twinkled merrily as he glanced her way.

"Let's replace this mask with a nasal tube, shall we?"

"Yes, let's," he said.

"Can he sit up, or does her have to remain flat on his back?" asked Sam.

"He can sit up for short periods if it doesn't cause more discomfort, but not too long at a time."

She went to the foot of the bed and raised him to a semi-sitting position then rearranged his pillows. "There, is that better?"

"Much."

His eyes rarely left Sam's as the nurse bustled about. She felt his impatience at the nurse's ministrations and could only hope he wouldn't stress out over it. That wouldn't be good at all.

"Thank God I'm rid of that damned mask. It was annoying."

Sam laughed. "That damned mask kept you breathing. Be thankful."

"So now that we're engaged, you're going to go all bossy on me, are you?"

"Going to? I thought I *was* the boss in this relationship."

"Ow! Don't make me laugh," he groaned.

"Sorry. Speaking of laughing, why did you find me reading so funny? I *can* read, you know?"

"Yeah, but I never took you for a romantic. Took me by surprise." He smiled and reached for her hand, but even that small effort caused him to grimace in pain. "My military mama has a tender spot."

"Yeah, for you. Maybe I should rethink that." She smiled to take the sting out of her words as she remembered his reference to her being a military mama when they'd first met.

"Don't you dare!"

"Don't go getting your shorts in a twist. I'm just teasing."

"I'm not wearing any."

"Oh!" The thought of him lying there in nothing but a Johnny shirt caused her heart to speed up and her pussy tingle. She tamped it down. Then she laughed.

"What's so funny?"

"Ah, in my hurry to dress this morning, I forgot to put on mine."

"Come here, woman!"

She rose to stand beside the bed. "Do you need something?"

"Yeah, you." He tugged on her hand and she leaned over. His kiss tasted sweet. Their tongues danced and tangoed to their own tune, but their kiss was short-lived.

He pulled back, gasping for breath.

"Blake?"

"I'm okay. Should 'a come up for air sooner, is all."

"Guess we shouldn't have done that."

"Hell no! The thought of your kisses kept me alive. I want all I can get."

"When you're better," she said, moving back to sit in the chair. "Would you like me to find something for you to read?"

"No, I think I'll just rest a bit. You staying?"

"Yep! You're stuck with me."

"Good." He smiled and closed his eyes.

She sat and watched him for a bit then picked up her book and resumed reading where she'd left off.

The nurse came and checked the machines, leaving as quietly as she'd appeared.

Sam hated hospitals. If it had been anyone else in that bed, she'd make her visits short and sweet, but it was Blake. She needed to be here–needed to hear him breathing, even though they were slow, labored breaths. He was alive. That's all that mattered. He'd survived the night and his prognosis for a full recovery was sound.

She confiscated a pillow and blanket from the nurses' storage cupboard and settled back in the chair to read, but her eyes soon drifted closed.

* * * *

Blake's road to recovery proved a long, arduous one. Complications set in after surgery, and he was not a good patient. The doctor quickly addressed the infection, but it meant a longer stay in the hospital. Sam spent so many hours playing gin rummy that she began to hate the game.

"Want to play strip poker instead?" asked Blake, his eyes glittering dangerously.

"We'll save that for when I get you home," she said, grinning at his pouting countenance.

"Which will be tomorrow, I hope."

She sat and studied him, this man she loved with all her heart. "Blake, you know I have to return to work. How are you going to manage?"

"You're not staying? You're the boss. Can't you just take an extended vacation?"

"I could, but I enjoy my independence too much to let things ride too long. Brogan is plenty capable to run things, but I feel I should be there."

"You won't do him much good as long as you're wearing a cast. When does the new prosthesis arrive?"

"I need to be in Calgary to have it fitted sometime next week, and I have the cast for two more."

"There you go, then. You can stay until the cast comes off, and I'll have time to figure something out."

"All right."

"What else is bugging you?"

"I'm wondering how we'll manage, you know, with me in Calgary and you down here."

"Once we're married, that won't be a problem. You don't really have to work. I make enough to take care of us both."

"Oh no! I need to work. What else would I do all day? Especially once you're back to work and off on assignment God knows where?"

"I've been thinking about that."

"And?"

"I'm quitting the force. They will probably need me to consult on some cases here and there, which I'd gladly do, but I want to work the ranch full-time. I didn't particularly enjoy getting shot."

"No, I don't imagine you did. I didn't have the choice of quitting after I got hit. They just ousted me on a medical discharge. Seems I wasn't any more good to old Uncle Sam."

"Sam, they knew you needed time to heal. Would you have gone back?"

"I don't really know, but it would have been nice to have a choice. *You* do. Take time to think about it, Blake. Maybe take a year's leave of absence and then see how you feel. This is a big decision. You need to make the right one."

"My horse ranch is beginning to see a profit. We might have a few lean years yet, but we could work together to make it a success. I know how much you love horses. What do you think?"

"Are you asking me to give up the shop?" Hope took root in her midsection.

"What if I was? Would you consider it?"

"Do you know how much I hate doing other people's dirty laundry?"

"No, you've never talked about it much."

"What's to discuss? It's not like raising horses or capturing killers. At least at the end of your day, you have something worthwhile to talk about…maybe even brag a little. Me, I do laundry."

"You provide a valuable service, but if you hate it so much, let Brogan run it for you. Stay with me."

"Brogan's talking about starting his own shop. He actually enjoys the work."

"Then why not sell it to him—be done with it."

She searched his face, his eyes, and saw the seriousness there. "This isn't because you need a nurse, is it?" she teased.

"No. It's because once they release me from this Godforsaken place, I want to wake up with you beside me every morning. I want to ride the range and muck out stalls with you by my side. Although, seein' as to how I'll have to do all the cookin' maybe you'll have to do more of the muckin' in exchange."

"Gee! That's supposed to encourage a girl to give up doing dirty laundry?"

"Yeah, is it working?" He grinned.

"Yes! I'll call Brogan tonight when I get back to Zak's and see if he's interested."

"Speaking of which, how have you been traveling? Did you replace your tracker?"

"Nooo, I haven't had time. I've been using your truck. I hope you don't mind."

He grinned again, his eyes full of merriment. "Taking liberties with my property already. I can see I'll have to keep a close rein on you."

"The closer the better. Got to go now, but I'll see you tomorrow."

"Drop by my place and rustle me up some clean clothes, would you?"

"Sure thing. I'd planned on it anyway. Can't have you walking out in your boxers."

* * * *

Sam left the hospital and drove straight to Blake's ranch. Unknown to him, she'd already moved some of her stuff in and tidied up the place in readiness for his homecoming. It would have been a lot easier if she had two good hands to work with, but she got the job done. Not without a few good bouts of cursing though. She might not be able to cook from scratch, but the grocery store in Fort McLeod had a well-stocked freezer section and bakery.

That was four days ago, and here she was back again. She parked the truck by the kitchen door and went inside. The first thing she noticed was a note propped up by the coffee pot. She giggled to herself. Someone sure knew them well.

Sam opened the note and read then read it again. It was from Zak. She put the note down and looked around. A huge fruit basket sat on the table amid various sized vases of flowers and potted plants…and chocolate! Cookie jars, filled to the brim, lined the counter with a cake tin at the end. She opened the cupboard doors to find an assortment of canned soups and packaged foods. The fridge had been stocked with milk, juice, cheeses, yogurt, and sandwich fixings. Sure enough, when she opened the deep freeze, inside was a mountain of casseroles.

A knock on the kitchen door took her by surprise. She opened it to see Zakia standing there, ushered her in and embraced her in a welcoming hug.

"Hi, Sam. I asked Blake's foreman to let me know if you showed up here tonight. I hope you don't mind."

"Not at all, but how did you get here so fast?"

"Actually, I'd just left and was on my way home when he called my cell."

"You didn't have to do all this," said Sam, gesturing around the room.

"I didn't. It's a neighborhood thing. We wanted to welcome you to the community and welcome Blake back. I didn't think you'd want or need to have the county dropping in on you, especially with Blake still recovering, so I arranged this little surprise."

"*Little* surprise? Blake won't have to cook anything for weeks!"

"I figured you'd see it that way as I know you don't cook, but the rest of the community doesn't. A woman has her pride." She smiled.

"Pride be damned! I can't cook, but I can sure tend horses. I'll earn my keep."

"I don't doubt that at all. Are you staying here tonight or coming back to our place?"

"I'll follow you home. Once I spend another night here, I'm not leaving, and I want to spend it with Blake. Kind of a new beginning for us."

"I understand."

"Just give me a sec to grab him some clothes for tomorrow and I'll be ready to go."

She ran upstairs without waiting for a reply and packed Blake's duffle, quickly returning downstairs. "That's it. Let's go."

"Got your keys?"

"Umm, they must be right here somewhere. There! By the coffee pot. I must have set them down to read your note." She grabbed them awkwardly with her fingers on the casted arm because she held the duffle in the other.

"Want me to take the duffle for you?"

"No thanks. I've got it."

"Now how did I know you were going to say that?" Zak teased.

Sam laughed. "You know me too well."

"Be happy, Sam. You deserve it."

Her friend's words jolted her back to reality with a bang. She couldn't marry Blake! In her anxiety over his getting shot, she hadn't once thought about her barren state. She had to tell him, had to break things off with him, but how?

"Sam! What's wrong? Are you all right?"

She looked up and saw the concern etched on her friend's face. "I can't marry Blake."

"What? Why not?"

"Look at this place, Zak. He built it for the family he hopes to have one day. I can't give him that."

"Oh, Sam. Have you told him?" she asked, putting a comforting arm around her friend.

"No. I've been so worried about him that it totally slipped my mind. All I concentrated on was being there for him while he recovered."

"And you have been. I think he will be okay with it. He loves *you*."

"I know that. I love him, too. It's just that I don't want to be responsible for him giving up his dreams and maybe regretting that decision a few years down the road."

"Then tell him and allow him to make that decision, Sam."

"Yes, I.know I should, but the doctor said no stress."

"Then wait and tell him when he's stronger. Either way, I think you need to cut him a little slack. It's you he wants…needs, right now. Be there for him and if it doesn't work out, what have you got to lose?"

Sam listened to her friend's advice, considered her words, and finally agreed. "I almost lost him once. This will give me a chance to store up more memories if nothing else."

"Think positive, Sam. It'll all come right in the end."

"I hope so, Zak. I certainly hope so."

She followed Zak home and went straight upstairs to bed. Exhaustion had set in big time, but her mind wouldn't shut off. When dawn lightened the sky, she was still lying there playing "what if" in her mind and not liking the outcome one little bit.

COVERT MISSION: UNDERCOVER COP

Chapter Fifteen

Dr. Forsythe showed up bright and early, and for that Blake was thankful. After he gave him his walking instructions, he'd signed the release papers and left. Breakfast came and Blake wondered where Sam was. He always ordered two coffees with each tray, but at this rate, hers would be cold by the time she arrived.

He finished eating, shaved in the miniscule bathroom, and then gathered his things for a shower, eyeing the brightly colored Johnny shirt with disdain. If he never had to wear one of those again, it would be too soon. Man, they were drafty! He penned a quick note for Sam and left the room.

The nurses he met on his way to the shower grinned widely as he walked by wearing nothing but a Johnny shirt and his black cowboy boots. This was the last time he'd be walking these halls, Lord willing. He might as well make the best of it. He tipped an imaginary Stetson at the ladies and exaggerated his cowboy swagger. They couldn't help but chuckle, especially when they saw his ass showing between the flaps once he'd gone by. A couple were brave enough to elicit a low whistle in response and one brazen little filly offered to wash his back. He laughed aloud, heartily enjoying the attention.

When he got back to his room, there was still no sign of Sam, and he picked up the phone to dial the ranch, having to replace it almost immediately when the nurse came in to change his bandage. She pushed open the curtain to leave, and that's when he saw Sam sitting in the armchair, his duffle at her feet.

"Good morning, beautiful! The doctor released me already so I'm good to go."

She smiled and rose to pass him the duffle. "You might want to get dressed first, but I wish I'd thought to bring a camera."

"Yeah, the nurses had quite a chuckle when I headed for the shower."

He ducked behind the curtain again and made short work of getting dressed. "You forgot my hat," he said when he emerged.

"No, I didn't. It's right there." She pointed to the side table on wheels that he used for meals.

"Good girl!" He slapped the hat on his head, feeling great for the first time since he'd been shot. He smiled at her. "Now I feel like a man again. Take me home."

"Yes, sir."

As they passed the nurses' station, one of them raised a hand to stop them. She came out brandishing an envelope. Blake took it and opened it to find a card inside with a handwritten message: Thank God you're gorgeous, honey! Having something nice to look at helped us overlook your obnoxious behavior." It was signed by all the nurses.

Blake laughed out loud. "Now, come on. I wasn't *that* bad."

The nurse grinned up at him. "Maybe not, but you weren't that *good* either."

"If I didn't have my loving fiancée to tend to, I'd show you what good is."

"Promises, promises. Take care." She waved them off and went back to her duties.

Blake felt sunshine on his face for the first time in almost two weeks. "It feels good to be going home. Hell, it feels good just to be outside. Hospitals are fine when you're sick, but I was ready to leave more than a week ago."

"Well you're out of there now. Come on. I'll drive you home."

        * * * *

Sam parked the truck in front of the house and turned off the ignition. She looked at Blake's home, its façade speaking a welcome she was far from feeling. Could she live this charade for another two weeks? How could she pretend everything was all right with her world about to fall apart? For Blake. Somehow she'd do it, for Blake.

He opened the passenger door, pulling her back to the present. The future could wait. She had now, today, and she'd enjoy it to the fullest. She joined him in front of the truck, and they walked to the house arm-in-arm. He took the key and unlocked the door, ushering her inside.

As soon as he'd closed the door, she was in his arms, being kissed like there was no tomorrow. Her insides melted at his touch, her panties grew damp. He pulled away, and she felt bereft.

"Let's go upstairs."

To bed? "What did the doctor say? Is it all right?"

"The doctor made me walk up two flights of stairs. He said if I could do that, I could make love. I did it without pain and without losing my breath and now, here we are. Come to bed with me. Don't make me wait a second longer."

He took her hand and guided her to the stairs. She was nervous, uncertain, afraid of hurting him, but oh, how she needed this…needed him.

They undressed each other in a flurry of flying clothes, uncaring where they landed. Sam hesitated again when she saw the bandage, stark white against his tanned chest.

"It's all right, Sam. I'm all right. Love me, please."

He lay down on the bed, and she went to him, kissing and caressing him as he kissed and caressed her. She straddled him and rejoiced as his cock entered her, filled her and she began to move, carefully raising herself up and lowering back down so as not to jostle him too much. He wasn't satisfied with that, soon pushing up into her with such force that she climaxed almost instantly. She continued to ride him with more vigor as the sensations traveled through her. Energized yet weak, aggressive yet controlled, it wasn't long before his juices spilled, mixing with her own.

"Damn! I forgot to use a condom again."

Should she tell him? Get it over with? She moved to lie beside him, her cast resting on his stomach as her fingertips stroked his heated flesh. With dread filling her very bones, she decided to tell him. It wasn't fair to put it off any longer.

"We don't ever need to use condoms, Blake. The accident…the doctor…he said I'd never…never have kids."

"Oh, shit! I'm sorry, Sam. Why didn't you tell me?"

"I couldn't stand the thought of you pushing me away."

He reached out a hand, tipped her chin up, and gazed into her eyes. "You thought I'd do that? Push you away because you can't bear my child?"

"Yes, I was afraid. This house was built for family, a big one."

"This house was built for love. What difference does it make if the children are our flesh and blood or orphans needing a good home?"

"Oh, I never thought of that. You'd want to adopt?" Her heart filled with hope.

"Sure, why not? But before we do, I intend to have you to myself for a while. Do you mind?"

"No, I don't mind one bit. I'm not ready to share you either."

She burrowed into the crook of his arm, an exultant smile on her face as she looked forward to a future filled with the promises of love…and horses…and children someday. But mostly, she gloried in the fact that she'd be spending it with the man she loved. Forever just didn't seem long enough.

The End

www.lorrainenelson.weebly.com

Evernight Publishing

www.evernightpublishing.com

www.ingramcontent.com/pod-product-compliance
Lightning Source LLC
Chambersburg PA
CBHW020631180626
46816CB00003B/917